T0321241

GOD-D

ISEASE

AN CHANG JOON

SARABANDE BOOKS
LOUISVILLE, KENTUCKY

Publisher's Cataloging-In-Publication Data
(Provided by Cassidy Cataloguing Services, Inc.).

Names: Joon, An Chang, author.
Title:God-disease / An Chang Joon.
Description: First edition. | Louisville, Kentucky : Sarabande Books, [2025]
Identifiers: ISBN: 978-1-956046-33-5 (paperback) | 978-1-956046-34-2 (ebook)
Subjects: LCSH: Identity (Philosophical concept)--Fiction. | Language and languages--Fiction. | Social norms--Psychological aspects--Fiction. | Names--Fiction. | Mind and body--Fiction. | Change-- Fiction. | LCGFT: Short stories.
Classification: LCC: PS3610.O64257 G64 2025 | DDC: 813/.6--dc23

Cover and interior by Danika Isdahl.

Printed in USA.
This book is printed on acid-free paper.
Sarabande Books is a nonprofit literary organization.

This project is supported in part by an award from the National Endowment for the Arts. The Kentucky Arts Council, the state arts agency, supports Sarabande Books with state tax dollars and federal funding from the National Endowment for the Arts.

CONTENTS

INTRODUCTION

"Now, I see places and people that I've never known," says a character near the end of this astonishing collection, "and I think that I'd be able to love them. . . . At least love better than what I know now." Such a statement, made with the characteristic straightforwardness that marks the style holding these stories together, is one that yields even deeper rewards on second glance. *God-Disease*, by the debut writer an chang joon, takes us into the hearts of characters who are ill at ease in their own bodies and minds. They seek solutions—or sometimes just the root of their problems—in their surroundings. Not only the physical landscapes (the municipalities of a new, contemporary Korea) but also the cultural notions that are passed down and maybe, for the first time, approached with serious doubt. What do these characters "know now"? More darkly, is *love* the right word for what we cannot see or know?

Many of the stories in *God-Disease* proceed with a deliberate pacing that can turn to foreboding before long. In the title opener, a young woman arrives from the United States to help curate a beetle exhibit at a small Korean museum. Her acculturation to her new surroundings lulls us, almost imperceptibly, to a psychic distress that charges her search for relief. In "Kuleshov Effect," the stultifying effects of a woman's trauma are nearly as harrowing as its origins, even as the details are never quite disclosed. "Context meant everything," the story tells us, insisting "that when two things were put together, meaning was divined." But how true is that in a world of slippery meanings and indeterminacy? In these stories, a 1990s dormitory is described already as "a relic from another time." In passing detail, a character's hair and manner of dress marks him as "a man stuck in a different time." "I just like walking through the museum and looking at all the curated things from across the world," says another character. "It reminds me that it's a real place that exists."

Cultural and historical change happens with such speed that

it can sometimes feel that art itself struggles to adapt to our time even as it tries to capture it. *God-Disease* showcases a writer adept enough to know already that not all transformations are renewals. Change comes, but what might come with it? "Something had departed forever," notes the beetle collector, looking at a specimen, "and left it a hollow vessel." All of the stories in the collection are inhabited with the haunting possibility that even rejuvenation might reveal that "we're all just filled with the wrong things." What a bracing, challenging book for a writer in early career, so brave in its willingness to unnerve—and move—us, by equal and astounding measure.

—Manuel Muñoz

GOD-DISEASE

GOD-DISEASE

Municipality J was too small for direct flights. I instead landed at Incheon and took a two-hour train. I tried to look out the window, but the sun had yet to rise, and everything was all shadows and indistinct shapes. I had been informed that someone from the museum would meet me at the station, but that was all I knew.

As it turns out, I didn't need to know more. Municipality J was not a popular destination. A woman was dozing against a beat-up

Subaru Legacy. Next to her was a crumpled sign that read *Dam Sun-bin Welcome!!*

"Hi," I said, then repeated myself when she did not wake up. "Hi. I think that's me?"

"Oh," she said, lazily stretching herself. "Was wondering when you'd get here. I'm Kim Seo-won."

She gave me an appraising once over.

"I thought you'd be a guy," she said. "Sun-bin is—"

"Often a guy's name. Yeah, I get that a lot."

I moved to load the luggage, but she waved me away, insisting on doing it herself. We initially drove in silence. I carefully took stock of her. She looked to be in her twenties. Her hair was dyed mahogany brown, but her black roots were showing. She drove with a confidence that bordered on recklessness, and I found my knuckles whitening as I gripped the handle over the door.

"So, what's the time difference?" she asked, breaking the silence.

"About fourteen, give or take."

"Wow."

After fielding several more questions, she brightened noticeably and began talking nonstop. I learned that she was a part-time at the museum, and that she initially only got the job to upset her father.

"But I really like it now," Seo-won said. "I don't know. I just like walking through the museum and looking at all the curated things from across the world. It reminds me that it's a real place that exists, that maybe I could even go there once."

She glanced at me then grew a little pink.

"Sorry for rambling. It probably sounds trite to you, dreaming about traveling around the world when you already do that for your work."

"Huh?" I answered, taken aback. "No, not at all. I don't think there's anything wrong with the desire to get away."

Perhaps flustered by her frankness, I also divulged something that I typically would not have. "Actually, I was born here. My mother too," I said. "Just the same as you. So it's not crazy to imagine that you could travel. I did it."

"Really?"

"Yeah, I—" A shooting pain ran through my head.

"Excuse me," I said as I reached into my bag. I fumbled around for several seconds. Another bright camera flash of pain split my head open and I gave up, dumping the bag entirely on my lap.

"Are you okay?" came Seo-won's voice.

"Just chronic migraine." I slipped the pills into my mouth and swallowed with no water. "Anyhow, yeah, I wasn't much older than seven or eight when we left."

"Is it any different from how you remember it?"

"I don't remember much, to be honest. Are you from here?"

"Born and raised. Never left," she said, then added, "although it wasn't for a lack of trying."

She didn't qualify her statement, and I felt awkward digging further.

She glanced at me. "You'll see," she said.

The museum had first opened in the late eighties—the fifties, if you counted its first incarnation.

"It burned down during the war," Seo-won said, unloading my bags. "Most of the buildings here used to be traditional wooden hanoks. All went up like a stack of matches.

"Luckily," she continued as she unloaded another bag with a grunt, "they'd moved the collection into storage before the air raids began. Once the war ended, they relocated here."

She pointed me toward the administrator's office. "It's on the right, just past the history wing."

It was a Saturday, but the museum was nearly empty. I walked past rows and rows of historic figures as they posed behind glass panels. A dusty group of Neanderthals gawped with glassy eyes at a burning tree. A sad excuse for a Genghis Khan sat atop his horse, a web of hairline cracks spider-webbing his sallow, sunken cheeks. An Imperial Japanese officer inspected the papers from a ragtag group of Koreans, a hand on the hilt of his sword. The paint was peeling from his fingers, revealing the tallow-white wax beneath. I walked faster. Their eyes set me on edge, although I could not exactly say why.

Even as I knocked on the door, all I could think about were

those effigies of wax. It was why, when the administrator offered his bloodless hand and introduced himself as Jeong-woong, my first impression was that he could have been an exhibit himself.

He was a man stuck in a different time. His white shirt, stiffly starched and entirely out of fashion, crinkled as he stood. His hair was thinning but jet black, that shade of shoe polish that could only come from a dye bottle. I could see a spot behind his earlobe where the spatter of dye had stained his skin black.

I nearly smiled and then felt unkind. I thought of my father, how he endlessly worried about his own balding pate.

Could you buy some of that hair-thickening fiber on your way back? he had asked, right before I left.

He said he'd tell me which one it was, but I didn't have to be told. We had a can sitting inside our medical cabinet for the past six years or so. There was a time, around two years ago or so, where I took the dusty and dented can out and asked my father if he wanted me to throw it out. It was empty—it had been empty for years. But he said no, and I asked why. I had a hunch but I asked anyway because I felt like being cruel and because I missed my mother. He hemmed and hawed for a while. All I eventually weaseled out of him was *She bought it. She*—a single-syllable pronoun. That was all he had been willing to voice. I imagined chucking the empty can at him, then imagined it bouncing uselessly off his chest. But the thought of him standing there, confused and sad in his striped pajamas, made me sad in turn and my eyes filled with tears and when he comforted me by saying, *You don't need her, I'm here*, I only ended up bawling harder.

I felt something wriggling and slipping out of my hands. My face grew warm as I realized that I had zoned out mid-handshake. Even worse, I had been gripping the man's hand the entire time. My head throbbed gently.

"Sorry," I blurted. "So sorry. Must've zoned out. I'm a bit tired."

"That's fine," he said carefully. "You must be jet-lagged."

"Yeah, a little. Anyhow, I'm so excited to be here. I look forward to the next year."

"Likewise."

We chatted for a while longer. Jeong-woong was not curt, exactly. He was not warm either. He seemed unable to make up his mind about me, vacillating between grudgingly admitting that his museum has seen better days and taking every opportunity to hint that his museum was just as impressive as any. It very quickly became exhausting.

Later, he offered to give a tour. I agreed, unable to find a polite way to turn him down. And so the two of us set off, the plastic wheels of my suitcase clacking loudly against the marble floor.

It was only when I came face to face with those waxy figures that I understood. It was the eyes that seemed to look everywhere. They reminded me of my mother.

◆

I left the museum and took a taxi to the apartment; I had already informed the landlord about when I'd be moving in.

"You must be Sun-bin," the landlord said. "Welcome!"

"Are you just moving apartments? Or are you from outside J Municipality?"

"Oh, I'm actually from America," I said. I explained that I'd be here for the next six months.

"You can take the 760A bus," the landlord said. "It's the blue one. And then two more stations through the subway. You'll get off right in front of the museum."

When I entered the apartment, it was small, bordering on drab.

"Guess this is home," I said.

I dropped my things off, then went for a walk around the neighborhood. I felt a little disappointed—it had the trappings of any other neighborhood in the States. I knew that it was a silly sentiment, but still the feeling persisted.

I found a couple of restaurants, one of which was even a passable imitation of a brunch joint. I went inside a 7-Eleven and marveled at how different it was. They had so much food—entire lunch boxes that could be heated and eaten there and then. I bought a small rice ball and a bottle of water. Nearby was a small park frequented by the locals. I sat on the rusted bench for a while and ate the food. There were children playing some kind of skipping game, one I did not recognize.

I walked on. There were several churches, all of them adorned with that bright, neon-red cross that I recalled from childhood. Two more convenience stores, a grocery, and a fish market of sorts. On impulse, I stopped at the grocery store and bought a bag of rice, and ingredients for kimchi fried rice. It was one of the few Korean dishes that I actually knew how to make. But when I got home, I realized that the only cooking appliance in the house was a rice cooker; I would have to just eat white rice and kimchi. I let the rice soak while I finished unpacking.

The rest of the move was surprisingly painless. Even with the jet lag, I did not find it exhausting. Afterward, as I sat by the dinner table and watched the peppery marinade of the kimchi stain the glistening grains of rice, it hit me. It was a Korean home; the floor was already clean. In the States, the first day of every move had been soaked with Lysol, with me scrubbing the floors until my head swam with that clean and strong smell.

"Home is where you can be barefoot," I said to myself, chewing slowly.

The next day, Jeong-woong and I discussed the details of my stay at the museum. We walked in a large, lazy circle outside the museum as we talked.

"It's my understanding that you will be curating a collection while you are here."

"Yes," I answered. "Specifically, beetles. I'm hoping to feature insects from both Korea and the States."

"How will you acquire the collections?"

"Some specimens will be loaned from my museum in the States. As for the rest, I'll either find and pin my own, or use what I can find from your storage."

"I am sure," Jeong-woong answered, his voice suddenly curt, "that you will find many good specimens within our storage."

I stopped walking, afraid that I'd offended the man somehow. But he kept moving as if nothing had happened, and I ran to catch up.

"When will the specimens from your museum arrive?" he asked.

"They should be shipped here within the week."

"If you need help unloading and setting up, please ask the part-time," he said. "We've also ordered some live insects for our terrariums, so if you could organize and home them when they get here, I would appreciate it."

He swiftly turned and walked into the museum. I grimaced as his figure dwindled.

Back inside the museum, I examined the office they assigned me. It was small and windowless, but clean. There were two rolling chairs and a wooden desk. On the wall was a painting—a replica Matisse. There were several pinned insect specimens, and I thought of my own collection that hung above my bed. Glass shelves lined the walls, the kind meant to display insect specimens, but most were empty.

The sound of something clattering to the floor made me turn.

Seo-won stood at the doorway, arms filled to the brim with various office supplies.

"Shit," she cursed. "Can you get that?"

I picked the stapler up.

"Jeong-woong asked me to get these to you," Seo-won said, placing them down in the office. "There's more, let me just go get them."

"Thanks, Seo-won," I said.

"No problem," she answered, turning pink again. She gave me an awed look then hurried out the door.

It took the better part of the morning to set up the office. After lunch, I started preparing the specimen, a jewel beetle with an iridescent carapace. Grabbing it with my forceps, I quickly dropped it into the kill jar and screwed the lid tight. The beetle immediately began convulsing, its tiny legs curling and uncurling.

"Woah," said Seo-won, her voice right behind my ear. I jumped.

"Christ," I said. "You scared me."

"Sorry, sorry," she stammered. "I didn't mean to."

I turned back to the jar. The beetle was dead.

"How does it do that?" she asked.

"It's a kill jar," I answered, as I fished the dead beetle out with the forceps.

"A kill jar?"

"It's an airtight jar with plaster lined on the bottom. You apply the killing agent and the plaster absorbs it. Drop the whatever it is you want to kill, screw the lid on, and done."

"What kind of killing agent?" Seo-won asked.

"They used to use cyanide. Some people still do, but that's rare now," I answered. "This one is ethyl acetate. The stuff used in glue and nail polish remover," I explained before Seo-won could ask further.

I placed the beetle on the table and flicked the ring light on. A tiny surgical table. I carefully made the cut. The scalpel sank into the abdomen of the beetle, right into the soft seam of flesh between the ridges of hard chitin. I wiggled the forceps into the incision and began pulling out its guts, soft and gray. The off-yellow blood stained the kitchen towel laid beneath the insect.

"I don't understand," Seo-won said, "how that doesn't gross you out."

"You know, back in ancient Egypt only high priests were allowed to make mummies. It was a position of prestige," I said.

"Yeah, but they worked with kings. You're pulling guts out of creepy-crawlies."

"Pharaohs, insects. What's the difference? I'd argue a pinning board looks prettier than a mummy."

I asked her to grab me some cotton balls. She complied, then hunkered down next to me, her face a mix of disgust and fascination.

"What's that?" she asked, pointing to the tub of powder.

"Talcum powder. It's meant to stop fungus from growing. It's not necessary with the smaller specimens but larger insects tend to have more—well, you can see."

I gestured at the small and neat pile of gray guts.

"It rots or molds," I said.

"You are so weird."

She said in a way that made me pause. It was mostly admiration, but there was something else there that I could not place. I made a mental note of it as I carefully began wedging the cotton balls into the now hollow insect.

"It really is weird, isn't it?" I spoke. "What I do."

"How do you mean?"

"The effort I go through to make it look like that."

"Look like what?"

"Alive."

I didn't believe in souls or spirits or any other ineffable essence that living beings might possess. But I had to admit that something was missing in this jewel beetle that I was cutting up. Something had departed forever and left it a hollow vessel—and me pulling out its guts had little to do with that emptiness. And once that happened, it took painstaking and careful effort for a now-empty thing to continue looking like an insect.

"Whatever was in here," I said, nudging at the carapace with my forceps, "is gone. And now I have filled it with surgery and anti-fungal powder and cotton balls."

A quiet settled between us. Distantly, I could hear a child crying in the museum, some kind of tantrum about being scared of the exhibits.

"Do you ever get the urge to bury them or something?" Seo-won asked.

"What do you mean?"

"I don't know, I guess just like to send them off."

"I think that'd get me fired," I smiled to let her know that I did not mean for the joke to be cutting. Seo-won blushed anyway. "I used to! Back as a kid."

"Why do you no longer? I mean you can't pin them all."

"True. I incinerate those."

Seo-won looked a little shocked. "That's a bit—a bit extreme," she said, then quickly added, "No offense."

"None taken. I just like things to be neat, I guess. If something has ended, it should end properly, no?"

It was partially a lie, but there was no way to explain. If I had it my way, I would have pinned them all. But that was simply not a possibility. I chose to burn the ones I could not pin, not because it was neat, but because it was over the quickest that way. Listening to hard chitin and soft pulp of the flesh hiss and pop within the flame was still awful. It was, however, *still* better than burial. To consign things to the slow, lingering rot.

I clocked out of work. Jeong-woong and others from the museum were going to eat dinner. I was invited; I declined.

"Still got a lot to unpack. That and the jet lag—you understand."

Thus left alone, I walked back to my house. After a bit of unpacking, I wandered outside until a restaurant caught my eye. The banner outside read *At Home: Homestyle Foods.*

Dinner ended up being rice, braised mackerel, and a bottle of soju that I could not finish. I had ordered the soju on a whim. It was my first day in Korea after all.

The mackerel's flesh was firm and chewy. It had a bright briny and savory taste with a faint sweetness that could only be detected by chewing slowly. My mother had taught me that.

It was a baekbanjip, one of those tiny holes-in-the-wall that served a rotating menu of homestyle dishes. Most of the other tables were filled with cubicle workers that came to unwind after clocking out.

The menu of the day consisted of either mackerel, pork belly on a griddle, or yukgaejang, a roiling pot of beef broth soup loaded with spicy chili oil. I chose the mackerel. Pork belly wasn't the kind of dish to order alone. As for the beef soup, I didn't want to embarrass myself by ordering something that was too spicy for me to eat.

"Are you from here, miss?" asked the owner. He was an aging man, with the wiry but hard arms of a man who was used to work.

I gave an answer that wasn't really an answer. "I was born here."

He nodded and turned to clear out a table. Later, as I paid, he handed me a cup of what appeared to be instant coffee. He gestured with his chin toward a machine near the entrance.

"Usually the coffee is self-service, but I figured you might not know how to use it. On account of you not being from here."

"How could you tell?" I answered. I felt inexplicably upset, a deer in headlights.

"Your Korean is very good, but I could still tell," he said. "And this is a pretty small city. New faces stick out."

Outside, I sipped the cup of instant coffee. It was cloyingly sweet, and I soon poured it all out into a sewer grate.

After dinner, I wandered the city.

I didn't remember much about J Municipality—it had been over two decades since I set foot in this city. What I mainly remembered from back then was the emptiness. J Municipality had been a part of the Korean government's failed efforts to renovate old neighborhoods. "Newtowns," they called it. Bulldozers had demolished all the plywood houses that cropped up after the war. High-rise apartments took their place. Then the people trickled in—never many, but a few here and there. They fled the rising rent prices of the capital, hoping that somehow the newness of J Municipality would translate to new opportunities. My parents had been a part of that anemic exodus.

The problem, of course, was that even though the apartments were brand new, there wasn't much to the actual city. It had been the government's hope that once people moved in, the business would follow, an idea that was woefully naive at best.

I sat on the bench where I sat earlier and recalled how my

mother would pick me up after preschool. It wasn't an everyday occurrence; only on Tuesdays, when the vet she worked at was closed. She'd speed down the newly paved road, me in the passenger's seat with the window rolled down.

"Ready?" she'd ask. "Here comes the underpass."

The car would slow and she would roll down her window as well. Together, we'd scream at the top of our lungs, hearing our voices echo and refract against the concrete tunnel.

"I want you to think of all the things that made you mad as you yell," she told me. "And that way, it's all out of you by the time we get home."

Our daily ceremony came to an end with the emigration. My mother was too busy adjusting to her new life.

One day, four years after the move, she suddenly asked me if I wanted to yell. We were on our way back from my band practice.

"Yell?" I asked, puzzled.

"You know, the yelling thing we used to do."

But I had outgrown such things by then.

I looked around at the park. The sense of emptiness was still here, but it was changed somehow. I looked at the narrow roads, at all the buildings crowded against each other. Illuminated signs covered the architecture. The building immediately across from me contained a piano hagwon, a dentist's office, and a realtor's office—one per floor. Many of the signs were off. Some were removed entirely, leaving behind only a rectangle of unfaded concrete. It finally hit me. The quality of the emptiness had changed. J Municipality no longer felt like an unoccupied place. Evidence of a busy city life was abundant—but that was all that was left. Evidence. The people had come and gone. A vacancy that suggested abandonment, rather than possibility.

"What happened here?" I asked aloud, then smiled ruefully. That was what I was here to find out.

Seo-won and I got along easily together. I sensed that she desperately wanted to be my friend. She somehow got the idea that I must be a rockstar scientist, to be able to travel abroad with such impunity. I would have corrected her, but she never directly broached the topic, instead opting for wide-eyed admiration. It made me a little uncomfortable; more than me, she liked what I represented. It was why I kept her at arm's length. We'd hang out during work or grab lunch together. Afterward, however, I made sure to keep my personal life separate from her.

"What happened here?" I asked once during lunch. "J Municipality. It feels a lot different than when I was here."

"Oh," Seo-won answered with a mouthful of rye bread and corned beef, "that's because of the harbor and the fishing boats. When did you say you left?"

"1996."

"Huh. Two years before I was born," she said.

I suddenly felt out of place. There was a strange, acute awareness of my age. Not old; I felt dilapidated. What was I doing here, talking with someone more than a decade younger than me? My entire journey to Korea felt silly. I was in my thirties. What was I doing? Still clinging to my mother? The ghostly echo of my father's voice rang in my ears. *When will you return to school and become a professor? Give up on your bugs and your mother.*

I must have been staring intensely at her. She coughed and averted her eyes.

"Anyhow," she said, "I'm sure you already know about the new town projects."

"Yeah."

She explained anyway, excited by the opportunity to demonstrate what she knew, and I couldn't help but smile a little at the youthful charm of it.

"So, the way they figured, if they made small-scale renovations, the rest of the town would still be old and dilapidated. Instead, they thought bigger. Look at the forest, not the trees and all that. Or, I guess, burn the forest in this metaphor."

I already knew, but I did not interrupt. I wanted her perspective. They had cleared the old villas and townhouses, sometimes strong-arming the locals to comply. The goal was to start anew, to wipe the slate clean and begin fresh. Noah with an ark of rebar and concrete.

"And then several big fishing companies built their harbor here," Seo-won said, rolling her eyes. "Including yours truly."

"You?"

"Well, my dad."

She sighed and took another bite of the sandwich.

"That meant jobs, which meant more people. More people meant more business. I'm sure all the government folks were thrilled," Seo-won said, her voice muffled by her full mouth.

"We even got some resorts and timeshare properties on the more scenic beaches. Things were looking real good for a while. Waterfront properties. Talks of a casino. Boat tours. A little slice of island paradise, right here in J Municipality. It's all the adults ever talked about—how once the bigshot investors closed the deal, they'd all make money hand over fist."

Seo-won laughed.

"What happened?"

"Overfishing," she said. "We stripped the ocean clean. The fishing boats began looking elsewhere—including the coastline where all the waterfront properties were supposed to go. The fishing companies wanted to expand and build more processing factories. They greased the right palms and got it done. Except nobody wants to go on a seaside getaway and smell fish guts all day."

She shrugged, sipping the water.

"There was a lawsuit. Several actually. It got ugly and the investors pulled out. We went back to fishing but—that ran out eventually too. We had picked the city clean. Municipality J simply had nothing more to offer. And when the money left, so did the people."

"Now you see why I wanted to leave," she said. "There's no future here."

We sat wordless for a while.

"Emptiness is our new national identity anyway," I said, and now it was my mother's voice echoing in my ears.

"What do you mean?" Seo-won asked, but my thoughts were distant. Quietly, my head began to throb.

It was back in 2002, the same year that Korea launched their new town projects.

It was only me and my mother that day. My father was in his final stretch of divinity school. We sat watching TV together in the living room, some history show playing on one of the two Korean channels that broadcast in the States. It argued that the quintessential Korean experience was urgency. Everything had to be finished *now*. Double the workload in under half the time. Expedited shipping became rush order which became same-day delivery. Wagons to steam engines to bullet trains, slingshotting us back and forth at lethal speeds.

After the war ended, Korea's GDP saw a hundredfold jump within a decade or two.

"The Miracle of the Han River, they called it," the host of the show said. "And our explosive growth was not limited to the economic sectors."

I learned that barely 4 percent of Asia was Christian, yet those numbers skewed wildly in Korea.

"Until recently, it saw a consistent growth of 9 percent a year," the TV said. "But why? It's because Korea is naturally conducive to cultivating impatience. It has four distinct seasons, with all the natural disasters that accompany them—droughts, blizzards, typhoons, and flooding. We have seen a plethora of invaders."

All of this, the host concluded, was what created this attitude.

"A sense of *now or never*," he said. "Korea adopted urgency as its mantra because we never knew what would befall us next."

"Nonsense," my mother snarled, and I jumped.

It had been a good day because good had become relative. Her mental state had deteriorated considerably. She had refused food and water, but she did not hurt herself or me. She did not hear the voices, or if she did, they weren't the upsetting ones.

"All this hurrying up," she said. "That began after the war. It's when they dropped the bombs. Wonsan, Chosan, Pyongsang. All reduced to soot."

She began pacing as one of her moods took her again. She crouched in front of the screen, her posture unnatural and stilted. Her back hunched and arched in a way that made me think of exoskeletons and bugs, some lithe, twitchy thing with a nasty bite. She began jabbing the image of the TV host. Her fingers made that dull thud, the distinct sound of flesh against glass.

"Gone. Blown to bits. And then along with the cities, all the things we used to believe in. Smithereens. You say a million and two Koreans showed up to listen to Billy Graham preach because Christianity saw explosive growth without saying why it exploded, don't you get it, it was all this hurry up, all this ppalli-ppalli."

She started rocking the TV with her hands, her voice rising to a rasping fever pitch. Somewhere amidst the shaking, the TV had unplugged. Still she yelled, spittle flying at the black screen that reflected her face.

"We needed to rush. But no wonder we had to rush. What choice did we have? We had an open wound for a worldview. Hollowness as our new national identity. The grandest psychological experiment ever, a return to tabula rasa on a national scale. We took our gods and crammed them into warheads—"

"—so that we could launch them at each other, that 38th parallel that separates North and South Korea isn't a border, it's the world's longest fucking rope that we've tied into a noose," I said.

I noticed that it was very quiet in the museum. Seo-won had vanished. I stood in a panic, my chair clattering behind me. What had happened? Had I said all of that out loud? Did I have a goddamn mental breakdown in front of a coworker?

My head throbbed viciously.

"Don't you start now," I said, kneading my forehead.

I kept my distance from Seo-won from that day on. I wasn't sure what she had seen, and I was too afraid to find out. It didn't deter her; she continued to haunt my office under various pretexts, or to ask if I wanted to grab lunch.

"No, thanks though," I'd tell her. "I'm just going to grab something from the convenience store."

At any rate, I often just skipped lunch, opting to roam the city. I didn't bother playing tourist. That's not what I was here for.

Instead, I made a list of all the fortune-telling houses, mudangs, shrines, and jumjip in the city. The first few times, I paced back and forth outside the buildings then slunk away, defeated.

When I finally gathered the courage to enter, I pushed the frosted glass of sliding doors to the side and walked in. But I found myself unable to talk. Much like that time with Seo-won, I was suddenly struck by the absurdity of my quest.

"Well?" the woman asked. "Are you here for a reading? Or perhaps to ask about marriage compatibility?"

She sat behind one of those low floor tables. Behind her was a shrine. Red was the dominating color. There were candles, along with many vases and bowls whose purpose I could not divine. Several statues dominated the walls, silent and imposing figures. Some held swords and spears, while others held flowers and fans. I quickly looked away before I could see their eyes. A strange feeling, one that I couldn't quite pin down, pooled at the bottom of my stomach.

I put my hand in my pocket and pulled out a photograph of my mother. I quickly placed it in front of her, concerned that my clammy fingers would damage the photograph. It was the only one I had left; my father had thrown out the rest.

The shaman studied the photograph, then me, puzzled.

"This woman," I said, stumbling over the words. "Have you ever seen her?"

"What?" she asked irritably, realizing I was probably not a customer. "This is a jumjip, not a private investigator's office. Don't waste my time."

She flicked her hand in dismissal and turned away.

"No, wait, please," I said. "She is my mother. She came to this city a long time ago to become a fortune teller—like you. I was hoping to find out what happened to her."

"I've never seen this woman," she snapped. "And I am not a fortune teller. I am a mudang."

She grabbed a folding fan that was on the table and slammed it down. I suppressed a flinch with some effort.

"Being a mudang," she said, enunciating each syllable, "means that I've got a god inside me. I commune with my god. I pray and make offerings. My god is my mentor, lover, and partner, all at once. It's not some cheap parlor trick like using your birth date and sexagenary cycle to make half guesses."

I tried to apologize but the mudang refused to listen. I found myself back outside, dazed and embarrassed. My head ached again, and the words of the mudang echoed in my ears. *Being a mudang means that I've got a god inside me.*

"Is that what happened, umma?" I asked out loud.

I was ten when a god entered my mother.

The god, however, was not benign. It was neither a guest nor a friend. If I had to describe it, it was more akin to a vagabond, insisting on squatter's rights.

It was August. School had started the week prior. I stood outside the bedroom door, my fingers curled around the straps of my schoolbag. The door did not open.

"I'm a little off today, Sun-bin," my mother told me. "I left breakfast on the stove."

"Okay, Mom."

"Banchan's in the fridge."

I remembered setting the table as well, although I could not remember what the dish had been. Some sort of soup, the broth cloudy. And rice—I remembered the glistening grains that stuck to my fingers. But that was only because I had picked the black beans out of the rice. I had eyed the bedroom door guiltily, but it remained closed.

Later, I broke a bowl while trying to wash it. The crack reverberated throughout the quiet house. I stood absolutely still, certain that my mother would come out of the bedroom to berate me—she always insisted that I just let the bowls soak instead of washing them. I stood there, rehearsing what I would tell her: *You were sick* and *I just wanted to help*.

Still the door did not open. I stood outside it for a while, trying to breathe soundlessly.

"Mom," I said. "I broke a bowl."

When no answer came, I tried to open the door. It was then that she finally spoke.

"Who's there?" she asked.

It made my skin crawl. Not the question itself, but her tone. There was genuine confusion to her voice, as if she did not recognize my voice.

"Umma," I said. "Umma, it's me, Sun-bin."

"Who's there?" she asked again.

I began turning the knob, afraid now. I wanted to see her face, wanted her to smile and tell me that it was just a joke.

"Who is that?" she said. "Who is that asking for me?"

I rattled the doorknob obstinately.

"*Don't*," she shouted.

I jerked my hand away from the door, as if it had burned me. Whoever was beyond the door, it did not sound like my mother.

"I'm sorry," said the thing beyond the door. "I'm sorry. Please just go."

"Did you find a church?" my father said on the phone.

I loved my father. Even after everything, I eventually figured out how. After all, when it came down to it, he had raised me while my mother had left.

But these occasions were the hardest, the times when it wasn't my father but Pastor Dam. He continued to speak.

"I asked around and there's a couple that are close to where you live."

"Yeah, I already found some," I lied unconvincingly, distracted by the results of my mistake—the latest batch of pinned insects had been ruined. I carefully lifted one to my nose. Rot, sweet and high, faintly drifted from it. I felt a migraine coming.

"Fuck," I said.

"What?"

"Nothing, Dad."

"Okay, well, if you haven't been, try going to Gwang-myeong Church or—" He paused, and I could picture him in my mind's eye, stooped over his phone to squint at a list of all the acceptable churches. "Heun-ri Central Church."

"What about Hwa-gok Church?" I asked, recalling a church I saw on my way to work. I had no intention of going to any church, but I didn't want my father to worry or nag.

"Which one?"

"Hwa-gok."

There was a pause, the sound of his phone keyboard clicking, then my father tsked.

"Probably not."

"Why not?" I asked.

"It's the wrong denomination. Hwa-gok is General Assembly

Presbyterian."

A small but insistent urge itched the back of my head, the impulse to ask, *What the hell does that even mean.* It was just the insects, I told myself. I was just angry because I left them outside and let the humidity ruin the specimens. I wanted it to be the insects; it was better than being angry at my father. Loving my father was work. It was work I knew how to do, but still work.

"And," he said then hesitated, "about your mother."

"Oh, yeah, I gave up," I said. The second lie was easy, well-worn, and left a bad taste in my mouth. "I asked around but no luck. It's just as well."

"Yes," he said.

I thought of my father's sermons and marveled at how much still clung to my memory. I knew that Samuel was but a child when God used him as a mouthpiece to talk to Eli, the elderly priest. I thought of Daniel and his exile, how he left as a young man.

Even through the phone, my father's relief was palpable. I would have considered it weak once; I would have resented him for it.

"I love you, Dad," I told him. "Don't worry, I'll be back before you know it."

When the search about my mother hit a dead end, I threw myself into work. There was plenty of it, anyway. Aside from the curated collection, the museum had not had a proper insect curator since the nineties. The storage was a nightmare of unlogged specimens and pinnings. Many were in poor condition, either molding or having rotted entirely. I didn't bother reporting it to Jeong-woong; I was sure he would take any criticism of the museum as a personal slight. I collected whatever was salvageable and re-pinned them. It was tortuously slow. Dried insects could not be moved and manipulated like freshly killed ones could. Wings and legs would fall off. Antennae would crumble. The dry specimen had to be placed in a relaxing chamber. A paper towel soaked with a solution that was equal parts water and rubbing alcohol was placed inside an airtight plastic container. The insect, then, was placed on a petri dish then placed within the container. After several days, the bodies became soft and pliant, having absorbed enough of the moisture. Then and only then could they be moved and re-pinned.

It was work, yes, and it was slow. But I was used to it. Because even as a child, I hoarded insects. In old photo albums, I could be seen with my fingers curled around mayflies and cabbage butterflies. I sometimes joked to my friends that being a curator wasn't a vocation—I just never figured out how to stop pinning things onto a board. When I was six, I got a biblical ass beating for trading my brand-new scooter for my friend's old ant farm. I snuck honey out of our cupboards and lathered it onto trees, then crept out at night with a flashlight to catch the moths and beetles that flocked to the scent.

My mother had been the more accepting one. She understood,

where my father only tolerated. I always believed it was because she had been a veterinarian back in Korea.

She bought me a terrarium and some field guilds. Together, we figured out how to keep my small captives alive. We learned what kind of sawdust a stag beetle needed, how to hold its chrysalis without injuring it.

I didn't understand it then, but it was never really about the insects themselves, or at least not solely about them. It was the change that captivated me. Because a larva and a chrysalis rarely looked similar—and what emerged from within looked entirely different. Although I did not have the words for it back then, the idea of such change was both thrilling and haunting: to become unrecognizable, even to oneself. And at the end of it all, a final transformation. Without exception, my little prisoners died.

When my first beetle died, I was convinced that it was yet another step, a point of stasis from which something even more amazing and marvelous would emerge. I let the thing sit in my terrarium for weeks, running downstairs to see what change, if any, the morning brought. It was only when it began to stink that my mother noticed.

"I'm sorry, Sun-bin," she said. "It's dead."

We buried it together in the backyard. We buried all our insects together.

Years later, when my mother cracked open like a chrysalis herself and vanished, I began to believe in prophecies. Not the ones in the Bible, the kind of prophecies where an Egyptian king or Nebuchadnezzar would be plagued by terrifying dreams and severed hands would write words on the wall. Those prophecies were grand and vast, interpreted by people chosen by God and spanning the fates of kings and kingdoms. My prophets were miniature.

After my mother left, I began pinning my dead insects. It was an exercise in futility. No preservation was perfect. Antennae and legs powdered and crumbled over time. Poorly dried specimens were overrun with mold. Even the perfect ones, pinnings that I exacted with excruciating effort, did not last. A year or two later, I'd open them up to see a fine layer of powder and grit lining the bottom of the board. Nearly invisible speckles of my effort, shaved off by time. I pinned them anyway. I wanted to defy this final change, to spit in the eyes of God—a tiny Dr. Moreau with her forceps. I did not let them return to the earth. Instead, I hung them on my bedroom walls. My insects only left with my permission and that permission would never be granted. Permanent and unmoving, they looked over me while I slept.

Although I found no traces of my mother, I continued to learn things about her. Although most mudangs deflated visibly upon realizing I was not a paying customer, some of them were kind enough to still talk.

"What, exactly, did your mother tell you?" a mudang asked.

"She said that she figured out a way to be cured," I answered. "And that she needed to go to Korea for it. To see a mudang."

The woman shook her head.

"It isn't something that you can be cured of," she said. "It's an illness, in some ways, but you can only accept or delay. You cannot weasel out of it, not if you truly have the aptitude to become a mudang."

She sighed, her eyes distant.

"Did your mother experience strange symptoms?"

"Strange? I—"

"Migraines? Phantom pains? Maybe she heard things?"

She told me that mudangs who had not been initiated suffered from shin-byeong, a god-disease.

"Let me guess," she said, with a small, bitter smile. "You take her to the doctors, who find nothing. Then you take her to a psychiatrist, who tells you it's psychosomatic. So you ultimately decide to hide her away in the house, ashamed of her like she's a lunatic."

What anger I felt was smothered by guilt. It was exactly what we had done. And although my father was the one who had led the charge, I had stood by, complicit.

The mudang sucked in air through her teeth, the sound somehow sympathetic.

"Poor thing," she said. "To come down with a god-disease, so far from her home and her ancestors. She must have been terrified."

My throat constricted, and I suppressed my feelings with

effort. I did not want to cry in front of this stranger. I opted for anger instead.

"What do you know about my mother and I?" I snapped, but there was no conviction there. The guilt was heavy, clinging to each syllable.

"I know that I was also once a scared woman, alone and confused," she answered. "A person suffering from a god-disease is like a house with a broken door. She had the spiritual aptitude, but no god of her own to protect her. If you are in such a state, you attract all kinds of spirits and ghosts. Unclean, malevolent things."

I thought of my father. His fury upon hearing my mother's suggestion. It was the only time I ever heard him curse.

"Are you fucking insane, Sun-wook?" he had shouted. "You think resorting to superstitious idolatry will solve this? Not to mention, what will the congregation say? Some fucking pastor I'd be."

But had Christ not driven out demons? What about the sermons he gave about the madman, the legions of demons driven out of him and into a herd of pigs? The mudang spoke again.

"If she came to Korea and looked for a mudang, it means she was looking to get a *gut* done."

"A *gut*?"

"A ritual. One that initiates you into becoming a mudang," she said. "To accept the god into you. And you need another mudang to be initiated."

I thought of my mother. *There is something special about me,* she had told me. *Not an illness, but a gift.* She carefully held her hands over her chest the entire time, as if something invaluable was contained within. It had been one of the last things she said to me.

"I don't know your mother," the mudang said. "But like I said, I was once the same scared woman once. I can offer a prayer for her, if you'd like."

"Oh," I said. And at that, the dam broke. My eyes watered in earnest. "Um, well—"

"It's not expensive," she said. "Just about 700,000 won."

I opened my mouth, but I was at a loss for words.

"Fine," she said. "500,000 won."

I left, strange and hollow.

The migraines steadily grew worse. I began taking days off, just to recuperate. Jeong-woong missed no opportunity to crow about it. He did not say it to my face, but everyone at the museum knew how he talked behind my back. He made snide comments about how being a big, fancy curator from the States was not all it was cracked up to be. I found him pathetic. Sometimes I almost thought about pitying him. But my splitting headaches made me irritable and tense. I lashed back, pretending to take calls outside his office with a friend.

"Shithole," I'd say, projecting my voice. "A rundown museum in a failing city. I mean I'll do what I can but sometimes you have to call it like how it is."

As my condition deteriorated, so did my work. I'd forget to take an insect out of the fridge, causing it to overdessicate. Other times, I did not add enough alcohol to the preserving solution. I clocked into work one day to find the specimen stinking and spoiled.

I sighed as I took the pins out of the specimen. The phone in my pocket buzzed.

How's it going? read my father's text. Then it buzzed again. *How's church?*

"Fuck," I shouted at my phone, bringing down my fist into the spoiled specimen. There was a tinkling sound as the petri dish broke. A wet sensation, hideously warm, bloomed under my fist. Then, behind my back, there was a second sound of glass breaking. I turned to see Seo-won, frozen in place. Near her foot was a broken beaker.

"Hey," I said, struggling to keep my tone neutral. "Sorry you had to see that. There's just a lot on my mind and I haven't been sleeping well."

Seo-won did not answer. Her hands were covering her mouth. She swayed there, as if dizzy.

"Hey," I said again, concerned this time. "Are you alright?"

"Miss Sun-bin," she said, her voice barely a whisper. "Your hand."

"What about my hand?"

The wet warmth persisted. I noticed, for the first time, a tickling sensation. Not exactly pain, but proximate. I looked down at my hand to see a rapidly expanding pool of red. Tendrils of blood mixed with the clear preservation liquid and unfurled into tiny flowers, millions of red blood cells expiring within the alcohol solution.

"It's just a cut from the glass."

Mutely, Seo-won shook her head.

I gingerly turned my hand over to see that one of the entomology pins was embedded into my palm, entering at an angle. The flesh curled and puckered where the two inches of surgical steel entered and left.

"Oh shit," I said, suddenly woozy.

"Don't worry," Seo-won's voice on the verge of tears. "I'll call an ambulance."

I felt a little like laughing at the irony of an entomologist getting impaled by her own entomology pin.

"Poetic justice, eh?" I said to the smashed remains of the larvae.

My head throbbed and my body went limp. I saw Seo-won dash toward me, crying in earnest. *What are you crying for, you silly goose. I'm the one with the hole in my hand*, I wanted to say, but my tongue felt heavy and fuzzy. Eventually, I quit fighting and let the comforting dark take me.

Surprisingly, the rest of the day was uneventful. I woke up at the hospital with a bandage wrapped around my hand.

"Nothing major," the doctor said. "Just a couple of stitches. Take your antibiotics and you should be fine. I'll write you a prescription for some pain relief as well."

He was halfway out the door when I called after him.

"Hey," I said. "Is it possible to get a brain scan?"

"Did you hit your head?"

"I, uh, no, this has nothing to do with—" I vaguely gestured at my bandaged hand. "It's a separate thing. I've been having these really awful headaches lately. I'm talking severe."

"You probably want a CT scan for that. I can direct you to the neurology department, if you'd like."

Awaiting my scan, I walked out to the lobby of the hospital to see Seo-won.

"Sun-bin!" she called out. "Are you okay?"

"Yeah, sorry that I caused you trouble."

I wanted to explain further, to offer some excuse for my behavior. To convince her that I wasn't crazy. Then I thought of my mother. *That didn't work out that well for her.*

"What'd the doctor say?" she asked.

"I'm fine, I'm fine," I answered. "Just have to take my antibiotics and I'll be fine. Listen, I figured that while I'm here, I'll just take care of some other business. I really appreciate you coming with, but you don't have to wait for me."

"Oh," she said, awkwardly. "Are you sure?"

"Yeah, you've already done more than enough. I can't ask you to stay further. I'm sure Jeong-woong will have your guts for garters already."

I walked back to the elevators, leaving a defeated-looking Seo-won behind me.

The CT scan itself did not take long, barely fifteen minutes.

"Well?" I said, getting up from the machine.

"The results won't be ready for a while," the doctor answered. "We'll take the scan and interpret it. The results will be in ten days or so, a week if we're fast."

"Oh," I said, disappointed.

"Don't worry about it," he said, brimming with confidence. "If there's anything wrong, we'll find it."

When I got home, I did not bother visiting mudangs. I didn't plan the curation either. I just sat on the pier with my legs dangling over the ocean. The sun was setting, but it was not picturesque. It looked more akin to drowning, the sun smothered by the gray, ash-colored waves. Nearby seagulls fought over a half-eaten fish carcass.

There was no way to tell for sure if my mother had become a mudang or not. I had no conclusive proof either way. But something in my guts told me it was true. Or maybe that was just what I wanted to believe. Because the alternative was too heartbreaking, to imagine my mother had left everything behind, only to fail at the end. I could picture nothing worse.

But of this, I was sure: She had seen the same sunset I was seeing now. My mother had loved the ocean in J Municipality.

My injured hand allowed me to take the rest of the week off; not even Jeong-woong had any objections.

I split the time between sitting at the park and visiting more mudangs. The latter, however, was a formality at this point. I had given up. It seemed like Korea had swallowed my mother whole, leaving not even bones behind. Still, I persisted. My logic was that the more mudangs I saw, the less regret I would have when I left J Municipality. Which was why I dedicated the final day of my injury leave solely to visiting mudangs; I didn't even bother eating.

It was nearly ten p.m. Most jumjips were closed, but I saw one with the lights on and decided to make it my final stop of the night.

It was brightly lit inside. The scent of incense permeated the room. Somewhere beneath the cloying perfume, however, was the persistent odor of old, waterlogged wood, a soft and gentle rot.

This mudang was a man. It was rare but not unheard of. This particular place had a thin curtain between the mudang and the visitor. To increase the intrigue, I assumed. The thin fabric obscured the man's features.

"Are you here to get your fortune read?" he asked. "Or are you here to inquire about compatibility with a partner?"

"No, I'm actually here to ask a question."

41

"Oh, you're her," he said, shifting his posture.

"I'm who?"

"Our community is a small one. Word gets around. I heard about the woman who went from door to door and asked about her mother."

"Oh."

"Would you like to perform a *gut* for her?"

"For what?"

"Well, if she's dead, we can lay her spirit to ease."

"You don't know if she's dead," I snapped. "And no, I don't need a *gut*."

"No, you wouldn't," he said. "I heard that too—that you don't put stock in mudangs. And yet here you are anyway."

He laughed, low and rattling.

"You people are all the same in the end," he said. "You're no different than my other customers."

"You don't know me," I said.

"No? I've been doing this longer than you've been alive. I can tell who is desperate. They crawl in here, stinking of divorce and dying parents and other catastrophes. Clutching at straws. At least they have the decency to believe in what I'm offering."

"Yeah, and then you defraud them," I said bitterly.

He suddenly slammed his fist onto the table, sending brushes and inkstones flying. As he continued to speak, his voice deepened and warbled in odd ways.

"You bitch. You stupid child. What makes you think you can question me? You think you can just show up here and ask your questions and get a neat little answer? Do you know all the things I've seen? The things that I've talked and communed with? How dare you."

"What the fuck is wrong with you," I said.

"I know what's inside me. Do you? Do you want me to pull out my guts and show you? Show you what squats inside me? If I did, you wouldn't run your mouth like that."

I backed away slowly, terrified. When I saw that he was beginning to rise, I turned and ran. I did not even bother putting my shoes on; I simply grabbed them and ran out the door.

"That's right, run," he howled behind me. "But you can't outrun your insides."

I ran without direction or purpose; all I wanted to do was get away. I could have run forever—or at least until I collided headfirst into something. I fell flat on my ass.

"Ow, fuck!" exclaimed the other person. "What the hell!"

I didn't waste oxygen by answering. I sat on the ground and took shuddering gulps of air instead.

"What the hell?" said the other person, more surprised than angry this time. "Sun-bin?"

I looked up. It was Seo-won, her face flushed red. There was alcohol on her breath.

"Oh," I said, my voice thick with relief. "Thank god."

"Is everything alright?" she asked.

"No, I just had a very strange thing happen."

"Hey, I was just drinking in a pojangmacha nearby. Why don't you join me."

I hesitated, but the fear from earlier on was still fresh in my mind.

"Sure," I told her. "I could use a drink."

A pojangmacha was liminality made architecture. It had walls, but it was mobile. Neon-orange tarpaulin sheets were supported by steel tent poles—and all of it could be removed and set up elsewhere.

Within, people crowded by twos and threes to exchange soju. There was no staff; the owner, the cook, and the server were one and the same. A wizened old lady moved with surprising dexterity as she delivered armfuls of steaming plates. Seo-won motioned toward a seat in the corner. I sat down, my hands gripping the handle of the stackable plastic chair.

"I was just drinking with a friend," Seo-won said. "But she had to leave early. Lucky for me, you showed up."

I laughed weakly.

"Yeah," I said. "Lucky, I guess."

I downed a couple glasses of soju, which calmed me down enough to retell what happened.

"What the fuck," she said. "That's fucked up. Did you report it?"

"Report it?" I asked. "I—no, I don't want to make trouble. Plus, I'm in a foreign country and all. I wouldn't know where to start."

"Well, that's not really true."

"What do you mean?"

"I mean you're still Korean. This is as much your country as it is mine. You said yourself that you were born here."

"Well, maybe."

Seo-won ordered more food, but I had no appetite. I stuck to drinking instead; soon enough, I could feel my words slurring. We talked for a while like that, about various things. Jeong-woong's shitty attitude. Some bill that was being passed to prevent over-fishing. How Seo-won was sad that I would not get to experience the Korean summer.

"Seriously," she said. "You have no idea what it's like. You could practically swim in the air, that's how humid it gets."

Despite my reservations about Seo-won, I found myself grateful for her presence. Her nonstop questions and comments were a welcome distraction. For the first time in a while, I found myself laughing.

"Yeah well," I said. "You haven't tried Boston winters."

"No, I haven't," she answered, then paused for a long time. "I suspect I'll never get to."

An awkward silence settled between us. Neither of us looked at each other, choosing instead to drink our soju. After a while, Seo-won opened her mouth.

"Why are you here?"

"You know why I'm here."

"No, really. Why are you here?"

"Because your boss has a frail ego and needs to simultaneously prove that his museum is good enough for a foreign exchange program but also prove that foreign museums aren't all they're cracked up to be."

"Ha ha," she said. "I'm serious. I want to know."

"I'm here to work."

"Come off it," she said. "You could've gotten a better offer. Be somewhere else. This?"

She gestured around at the small crowd of drunks.

"This isn't where you are going to make your career. You had options."

My head began to hurt again. I drank more soju; it was easier than answering.

"I can tell," Seo-won continued. "Matter of fact, I'm the only one that can tell—because I'm just the same."

"Same how?"

"Like I said, my father owns one of the major fishing companies here. I can't figure out a way to say this without sounding like a dipshit, so I'll just say it straight—our household is one of the few rich families left."

"Wow, congratulations," I said drily. "What a crowning achievement."

"Don't be shitty. I'm just saying that I had options. I could have just done what my dad wanted. I would have had stability. A place to call home. A family that might not understand me, but still loved me. I instead chose this. If you have a choice, you have a reason. What's yours?"

I was quite drunk at this point. More soju would have been a bad idea. I drank anyway.

"What did your father say?" she asked, then chuckled. "Oh man, I thought I pissed my dad off by waiving my rights to the family business to do this. You did a cross-continental dip out, all because you wanted to!"

Her voice dripped with rueful admiration.

It's not like that, I tried to say, but my tongue was tripping over the words.

"Come on, what'd he say?" she asked again. "Did he cry or shout? They all either cry or shout. Sometimes, I think that's all they know how to do, Korean fathers."

I grit my teeth.

"He was fine," I carefully said.

"Really? And your mom?"

My jaw popped.

"Ah, so it was your mom for you," Seo-won said. "The way it was my dad for me."

"No," I said. It was all I could manage. I thought about punching Seo-won, right in her smug fucking face.

"Come on, you can tell me. What'd she say?"

"You said earlier," I spoke, each word a struggle, "that you also had a choice but chose this. Why did you choose this?"

I did not give her a chance to answer.

"Let me guess. Because you're a spoiled little bitch who wanted to prove she's got real grit. That even though you were born with a silver spoon lodged up your ass, you didn't need it. You think I moved from America to here, just to thumb my nose at my parents? What do I look like, a child?"

Seo-won stared at me, mouth slightly agape. I continued to ramble.

"You wanted to know what my mother said? Nothing. *Nothing.* You know why? Because she went insane when I was ten, and then abandoned me a couple of years later to come here and become a fucking mudang. That's what I'm here for. To figure out whether she lived or died."

I stood up, the violence of the motion rocking the cheap PVC table and sending the silverware flying. I snatched up my bag, fished out my wallet, and threw down a handful of bills.

"Seo-won," I said, "I think that the only thing that you and I have in common is that we're both fuckups that disappointed our parents. At least I have the excuse that my parents were also fuckups. What excuse do you have?"

I turned and fled into the night.

◆

Seo-won kept clear of me after that.

I stopped seeing mudangs. I clocked in to work, prepared the exhibits, and left at six p.m. My headaches grew worse, and sometimes I even lost time. But it was alright because no one was there to witness it.

The CT results were in.

"I'm not sure," the doctor said. "The results seem pretty normal."

I marveled at how different he seemed from the first time I saw him. He looked so useless, a small lump of a man in his white lab coat, stethoscope slightly askew.

"You remind me of Dad," I said.

"What?"

"I said you remind me of Dad," I repeated, this time realizing I really had said that out loud but too tired and in pain to care. "He looked like that whenever Mom had one of her fits. So well-intentioned and useless. Do you think Eli looked like that?"

"Eli?"

"A priest. A good man with evil sons. The Lord broke his neck for his children's sins. It's funny how that works. Did you know that after Abraham tries to sacrifice Isaac on behalf of God's command and God stops him, Isaac never talks to him again? Genesis 22. The climb to Moriah. The last thing Isaac ever says to Abraham is *Dad, where's the sacrifice.* I hate quoting scripture, but it's got so many interesting stories. Anyhow, having a parent. Having a child.

It's a zero-sum game of a relationship, isn't it? Don't you think so?"

My own father never raised his voice with my mother, not until the end. Aside from that final, furious fight, he did not swear or shout. He simply implored. It was why, I think, that I managed to forgive him for letting my mother go.

"I couldn't help it," I said. "He just looked so helpless and sad."

"You know, I can refer you to someone you can talk to," the doctor said after a long while. "I think you need someone to talk to."

"What about my headache."

"As I said, based on these CT scans, I think it might be psy—"

"Psychosomatic," I finished, my voice dull and hollow. "Like her."

"Like whom?"

I got up to leave.

"I really think you should consider talking to someone. It might help."

"Thanks, but I don't think it'll help," I said. "It didn't for her."

"Who is this *her* that you keep mentioning?"

I walked out of the clinic instead of answering.

The clock read nine p.m. There was a hoesik today, where everyone from work left together to eat and drink. I volunteered to stay back and check on the live exhibits. No one disagreed. Some even looked relieved. I could have just clocked out, but the idea of tossing and turning sleeplessly was worse. It was why I now sat alone in the dimly lit insectarium hall.

"Come on," I said as I peered into the tank. "Where the hell are you?"

Rhino beetles had a habit of burrowing into the ground at night. I was checking them for parasites. The males, with their protruding horns, were discovered easily. The last female, however, continued to evade me. I shifted the dirt around; the low hum of the heat lamp buzzed in my ears.

"It's for your own good, you idiot."

Something clattered behind me. I glanced back, but the lights for the rest of the museum were off.

"Who's there?" I asked, one arm still in the terrarium.

For a brief moment, I heard an echo of my mother in my question. I suppressed a hysterical yelp. *Calm down. Calm down. Calm—*

There was a bright flash of pain.

"Ow, fuck!" I yelped, jerking my hand out of the beetle tank.

Still attached to my hand was the last beetle, its sharp pincers wedged into that soft wedge of flesh between the thumb and index finger. The same hand that I injured earlier that month. Two trails of thin blood ran down from the tiny but deep puncture wound. I swore again, but there was no time to worry about beetles. I tore the thing off my fingers and threw it back in the terrarium, my heart still racing.

"Who's there?" I asked again, peering into the looming shadows of the exhibits. "I have pepper spray."

I didn't have any such thing. For a fleeting moment, the childish urge to pray struck me. I did not give in.

"Stop it, Sun-bin. Like that's ever helped anyone."

I instead grabbed a mop lying nearby, taking care to avoid using my injured hand. I took a deep breath and made a run for the light switches in the atrium. The sound of my running thundered throughout the empty museum. Was that a second set of footsteps following me, or was that just me? I pumped my legs harder, wheezing.

I hit the switch. Light flooded the museum and I blinked at the sudden brightness. I cautiously walked toward where I heard the sound. Upon seeing what happened, I squatted and shuddered in relief. It was just a wax statue that had tipped over: a Korean war veteran clutching a rifle. His face was blackened with what I assumed was supposed to be soot. It was contorted in an expression of anguish. I once again found myself avoiding his eyes.

A jolt of pain wracked my head, and my bitten hand throbbed, as if in response. I looked down and recoiled. The beetle's head, torn clean off from the rest of its body, was still attached to my hand, its mandibles lodged into my skin. Twin jet-black eyes peered at me in accusation. I felt sick. My trickling blood oozed down and mingled with the greenish-yellow fluid that leaked from the beetle's head, soundlessly spattering onto the floor. I tugged at it, but the thing held on, refusing to let go.

Finally, with a small grunt of pain, I ripped the head off my hand. I walked back to the terrarium and plucked the other half out of the dirt. I knelt on the floor, holding each one in my hand.

"I'm sorry," I said. "I didn't think this would happen."

"Isn't that what you said last time?" asked a voice.

It was the severed head.

I froze. Before I could do anything, the mandibles opened wider and wider, the exoskeleton cracking in protest. In the center, there were teeth instead of the delicate feelers that would normally be there. They were square and blunted, like those of a human. I could not move. The head let out a chittering laugh. Its teeth clacked.

"Isn't that what you said?" it asked. "Right after you fucked it all up?"

The body of the beetle began to twitch. I tried to scream, but the air had been sucked out of my lungs. As I sat transfixed, the body turned to face me. A tiny, bland human face emerged from the severed stump.

"I mean, what's a measly bug compared to your parents?" the head asked. "Your father?"

The tiny head drooled and contorted, changing into my father's face.

"Sun-bin?" it asked. "I need you to pray. For your mom. For this family. We're all relying on you."

"He lost one family member and yet here you are, leaving again," the head said. "Look at him blubber, the poor thing."

Green insect blood seeped from my not-father's eyes. I wanted to vomit. Still, I found myself stuck in place, pinned like one of my insects.

"Not to mention your mother."

The face on the body groaned as its features warped once more. A low moan of terror escaped me. Long hair began sprouting from the miniscule scalp. Soon, it became a tiny imitation of mother's face, its eyes wild and rolling.

"Sun-bin?" it asked. "Don't worry. Umma figured it all out. There's a god inside me. I just need to go to Korea, need to go back. You understand, right? Your dad doesn't, but you do. Don't tell Dad. It'll be our secret for now. Umma will be back when she's okay."

"And you did, didn't you?" the head accused. "You kept her secret. You knew that she was going to leave, weeks and weeks before your father did. And you said nothing. You did nothing."

"No," I whispered. "No, I didn't think this would happen. I just thought—"

"He could have stopped it. But you didn't tell your father and then it was too late by the time he found out. She was gone."

"I thought I was helping," I said. Some detached part of me noticed the tears running down my face. "Mom asked me. Mom asked. I just wanted her to be okay. Mom asked."

"And now here you are, trying to find out whether she's become a mudang," the head said. "But aren't you really just trying to soothe your guilt? To tell yourself that you did the right thing by letting her leave?"

"No, I didn't come here to—that's not. I didn't want her to leave."

"I understand. You tired of them," it said. "Your relentlessly religious father. Your mad mother. You wanted it to end. Well, it ended."

The face on the body of the beetle began to change again, its features a mishmash of my parents and a beetle. A cacophony of mandibles, human features, feelers, chitin, and bone that clacked and drooled. Both the severed beetle head and the body of the beetle started to speak in tandem.

"And here you are now, a product of both," they said. "Who knows what's lurking inside you? You are your mother's daughter after all."

"Stop," I said, then begged. "Stop. Please stop."

"Who knows what you've inherited? What lines the inside of your guts? What has piled up under your bones? Shall we find out?"

With the suddenness of a snapping tibia, my body returned to me. I smashed my hands onto the floor, crushing its contents to a paste. Sharp chitin tore my palms to shreds, but I continued to smash my hands until they were bruised numb.

Then I turned and ran.

I saw a wet sun, wet like the snails I raised in fourth grade, snails never appealed to me because they had everything at once, their softness encased in a shell and they did not change, they were born like that, how could one truly trust a creature like that, one that was made then presented itself to the world and said *here i am complete and finished,* one that says *i will remain as such until our sun burns out.*

"Read my fortune."

"I need your name and—"

"Just fucking read it."

The sun was rising over the gray ocean, gray as the ashes of my grandmother, which I'd never seen but we were sent a photograph of them after her cremation, my mother cried for weeks after that, I thought she'd never be the same afterward, funny because I was right and wrong at the same time, she would never be the same but my grandmother's death was not the decisive event, it was just like an insect, a larva into a chrysalis into an adult into a dead thing that no one wanted, when my mother became what she became, I thought that she would make yet another transformation but she instead became like the dead beetles that bloated and stank, then disappeared.

"So you said your name was Sun-wook?"

"No, that's my mother's name."

"Okay, so what's your name?"

"Just pretend that my name is Sun-wook and read my fortune."

"That's not how this works."

"Please.　　Please　　please　　please　　please pleasepleasepleasepleasepleasepleasepleaseplease."

A crowd of seagulls fought over the remains of a dead mackerel, they tore its innards out, the fish stared into nothing, I ran and joined in, I wanted to take instead of having things taken from me, just for once, I did not want to be helpless and sad, stinking fish guts piled up beneath my fingernails but that was okay, hieromancy was an ancient practice favored by Etruscans and Greeks where they would take a ritual sacrifice and use its guts to interpret the future, I was sick of not knowing, I no longer wanted play Nebuchadnezzar, I wanted to divine, even if I had to tear it out of someone, even though I did not know how to read guts it was still fine, it was satisfying to hollow something out, to gouge, I wanted to predate, I wanted to play god, because there was an inherent violence to becoming a vessel—something always had to make room, something had to leave before something else could enter, whether that be gods, dead relatives, or a way of living.

I became distantly aware that someone was talking. Eventually, I realized it was me.

"I think I need a *gut*."

I drifted. I floated and sublimated, I moved ever upward. I thought of Elijah and how he was whisked away to heaven. But there was no chariot of fire waiting for me. Instead, when I looked down, all I saw was my grubby apartment and my body.

She gathered the insects that she had already pinned, then smashed the glass casing open. She took fistfuls of entomology pins, seemingly unaware how they stabbed at her already bleeding hands. She drove pin after pin into the insects; the abuse made their delicate bodies burst. Talcum powder flew about the room, dancing in the anemic dawn sunlight. Still, she continued to impale, over and over again, a weeping Pilate and a chitinous Christ. Throughout it all, she kept whispering, first in English, then in Korean—all of it nearly unintelligible from how hard she wept.

"Please don't leave," she said. "Please don't leave, umma. Please don't."

When I woke up, I was in my apartment. The ruined remains of my preserved insects were strewn around. My limbs ached as if I had run a marathon. The clock on the wall read two, but I could not tell whether it was night or day.

I checked my phone to discover utter pandemonium. The administrator had sent over five texts. Seo-won had sent a couple. My father sent over twenty messages and called five times, even though it must have been early morning in the States. The last one read: *please please please come back. don't do this. i can't go through this again.*

I scrolled up the phone and read what I sent him.

Dad, I think I am going to get a gut done.

I did not read what he sent me; I did not dare. I instead turned the phone off and laughed quietly. It made my head hurt, but I did it anyway.

"I'm lonely, umma," I said. "I don't have a single person who understands."

Tears blurred my vision.

"I guess this is how you felt, umma."

I did not return to my apartment or the museum. I instead stayed at a cheap motel. At night, I went to the restaurant I always went to and ordered mackerel, then drank soju until I could barely stand.

During the day, I roamed J Municipality, looking for a mudang that would help me with the *gut*. It was not easy. Many charged a fortune. Others refused on the basis that I only wanted to get the ritual done and not become a full mudang. Still, I persisted.

She did it, I kept telling myself.

She did it, and so could I.

Eventually, even when I did find a willing mudang, there were more hoops to jump through.

"I can't do it immediately. You'll have to wait two weeks, at least. And the week before you get the *gut* done, you shouldn't do anything spiritually unclean."

"Unclean?" I asked.

"No bath, no sex, nothing that involves blood. Make sure your period doesn't fall within that time span."

A small part of me rebelled at the mudang's words, the same part that defied my father and his sermons. But I was tired. I nodded.

"Also, just so you know—you can accept the god, or suppress it," the mudang said.

"Suppress it?"

"Well, it's called a suppression, but in truth, it's closer to postponing. You only become a mudang if you accept the god."

"What happens if I postpone?"

"It'll eventually return."

"What does that mean, eventually?" I asked.

"Could be half a year. Could be seven years. I've seen both," she answered.

I thought of my father's face—not my real father, but the thing that had sprouted out of the beetle's severed body. My head began to ring, and nausea, as visceral as the one I felt that night, filled me once more.

Neat. I desired neat things. I had failed to preserve anything. Our family. My mother's memory, even my sanity. Better to burn it all down. Reduce it to cinders so that something else can take its place. I did not want to linger or doubt.

"I want to be a mudang."

I called my father. I had always intended on telling him, but only after it was all over. But his final text broke me: *I deserve to know. Even your mother afforded me that much.*

I waited until the day of—right when everything was set up for the *gut*, when it would be too late for him to stop me. I was dressed in the traditional garb for the ritual, the fabric heavy and foreign against my skin. My fingers, slippery with coppery sweat, fumbled with the phone. It was nearly three a.m. in the States but he still picked up.

"Dad, it doesn't matter what you say, I'm getting the *gut*."

"Like your mother?" He snarled, barely sounding like himself. "A lot of fucking good that did her."

"What do you mean?"

"She got the *gut* done," he said. "She wrote me a letter afterward. And guess what—she was still crazy. She still heard things. A year later, she died in a hospital."

"I don't under—"

"Your mother had a prion disease," he shouted, his voice hoarse. "She had a prion disease. There was no god."

"What?"

"A prion fucking disease," he shouted. "A misfolded protein. That's all it was. The hospital sent me the fucking letter with the test results."

I swayed in front of the building. Beyond the wall, the *gut* had already begun. Loud music filled the air, traditional Korean instruments that beat and clanged discordantly. It soon rose to a fever pitch. All I had to do was take one more step. Cross over the threshold.

"Sun-bin," my father said, no longer shouting. He wept instead. "There was nothing for your mother there and there is nothing for you there now."

I ended the call. I recalled the watery sunset at the pier, how I thought there could be nothing worse than my mother traveling all the way here and failing to get her *gut*. But I had been wrong again. It could always be worse.

"She did get the *gut*," I said to myself. "And it didn't help her. She did get the *gut* and it meant nothing. She abandoned us and we abandoned her."

And none of it had meant anything. If I could have cried, I would have. Such things were beyond me. I stood there and hurt instead. I looked down at myself, at the ritual garb that weighed my body down.

For the second time, I turned and ran.

I sat in the American brunch spot, my plate of pancakes cold and untouched. I had thought of going to the restaurant I always went to, but I never wanted to eat another plate of mackerel. A pair of feet stopped at my table.

"Do you mind if I sit here?"

It was Seo-won. I did not answer. She sat anyway.

"Are you going to eat that?" she asked. I shook my head numbly. She pulled the plate toward her, drowned the entire thing in syrup, and began forking chunks of soggy pancake into her mouth.

"You know, you caused quite the stir at the museum," she said. "To be honest, I think Jeong-woong was kind of happy, deep down.

He got to feel superior to a bigshot from America. I think you proved everything for him, that he's just as good as anyone from over there."

I still said nothing. I don't think I could have said anything, even if I wanted to. I was devoid and spent.

"You know, you shouldn't keep all of that pent in," she said. "It can't be healthy."

"How could you help?" I said quietly.

"I can't!" she said, then smiled, syrup on the corner of her mouth. "But maybe that's why you should just tell me anyways."

I leaned back on my chair with exasperation. Around us were groups of three and four, all parents with children. They sat in red-and-white booths, a poor imitation of a fifties American diner.

"You know, I thought a lot about what you told me last time," she said. "And you're right. Maybe we're just both shitty kids who disappointed our parents. But that was kind of a load off, you know? I'm done trying to impress you. I've just decided to talk to you as someone I've met. Someone that, by all odds, I'll never see again once you leave this place."

She pointed at me with the fork.

"Try doing the same. I'm just some nobody who will never leave this bumfuck nowhere town, someone you'll never see ever again after you leave here. When you leave this restaurant, I'm gone. What I think doesn't matter. Now," she said, returning to her meal, "I'm curious. What's ailing you." She wagged her fingers.

"Pretend like I'm one of those mudangs you've been searching out. I've got all the answers. All you need to do is ask the right question."

"It's not that easy," I said. "And my problem is less about the right question and more asking the right person."

"Who is the right person to ask?"

"Not you, that's for sure."

Seo-won ate a bit more in silence then nodded in acknowledgment.

"Fair enough, how's this then," she said, then turned the chair around so that I could only see the back of her head. "Now I really might as well be anyone."

I laughed.

"Aha, see? You laughed," she said. "Now say your piece. You could even say it in English. I wouldn't understand a word of it. I'll just sit here eating your pancakes."

I sat and stared at the back of her head. I thought about just leaving, then thought about what awaited me in my apartment— my ruined insect pinnings strewn about in that small room, now somehow horrible and cavernous.

"I guess we're all just filled with the wrong things, umma," I said. I began in English but switched to Korean.

"You and me both. Maybe you really were pointless and empty, and there was nothing inside you, no God or gods or spirits. Maybe the only thing you really had were some misfolded proteins in your brain, and that's all you left behind for me."

I deliberated for a moment.

"I mean, in a really shitty way, now I understand," I said. "I now understand how you felt. How scared and lonely you must have been. Maybe that's all you needed, for someone to look at you and say, I understand. I understand you. My only regret—"

I caught myself and laughed.

"Okay, that's a lie. I have a whole lot of fucking regrets. But my biggest regret is that I never got to tell you this."

I took a deep breath.

"I forgive you." I stared at Seo-won's head for a bit longer. "I think that's all."

Seo-won did not turn around.

"You switched to Korean," she said.

"Yeah, well, I only really started learning Korean after she left, so she never saw how good I got. I wanted to show her."

Seo-won did not ask who I was referring to, which I was grateful for. We sat like that for some time: me staring at the back of her head, her slowly eating my pancakes.

"You should go," she said eventually. "I'm just going to finish this."

I complied. I walked to the entrance and paid the bill. I glanced toward Seo-won, but she had already turned her chair back around. All I could see was the back of the head.

"Hey," I said, projecting my voice. "Thanks."

She waved instead of answering.

◆

My apartment was a wreck. I did not take my shoes off; there was broken glass everywhere. I sat on my bed and called the museum.

"You're goddamn fired," Jeong-woong immediately said upon picking up. "Absolutely fired. I'll make sure that you never find work again, Korea or otherwise."

Seo-won had been right. Satisfaction lurked in every syllable.

"I'm sorry," I said. "Seo-won told me what happened, but I wanted to apologize in person."

"Who?" Jeong-woong demanded. "Who the hell is Seo-won?"

"The part-time," I stammered.

"You're crazy," Jeong-woong said, voice thick with disbelief. "I actually hired a crazy person. An actual, genuine lunatic."

"Seo-won," I said. "She picked me up from the airport."

We don't have any part-times by that name. You took a taxi on your first day, was all he said before hanging up.

"Oh," I said.

I began to laugh. I couldn't help it. A real from the gut laughter that took ahold of me. The first of its kind I had in Korea. I laughed until I was wheezy and hoarse, tears of mirth welling in my eyes. Then, I thought of the first time. The very first time a god entered my mother. For over two decades, I had turned that moment over and over again in my mind. How frightening her voice had sounded. For the very first time, I thought of the food on the table. The rice in the rice cooker. The soup in the pot, still warm. She, despite everything, had dragged herself out of the bedroom to cook that breakfast for me. My mother.

I carefully gathered my ruined specimens and took them to a nearby field. I began digging a hole with my bare hands. The effort stung my injured hand, but it was pain that I did not mind. I carefully laid them in the ground and tightly packed dirt over them, digging a new hole for each insect. I found the work surprisingly exhausting, and soon I was sweating profusely.

I finished my burials. I slowly stretched my limbs. No gods, prophesies, or visions filled me. I sat there, hollow and serene.

KULESHOV
EFFECT

It happened while Jung-ha was dressing for work. A soft and muffled crack, followed by a swollen belly of a silence that loomed, distended and horrible. Her pulse thundered in her ears, offbeat and tinny, as if her heart had been swapped out with a faulty metronome. She felt her arms falling slack, hand still clutching the hair dryer as it blew air onto her leg.

She walked into the kitchen, already knowing what she would

see. There was a dark stain on the carpet, growing wider by the minute. Lying on the stained carpet was something that had once been a teacup. It had split down the middle. Jung-ha knew where the cup had been; she always remembered where she put her cups.

She mopped up the tea but did not sweep the floor. There was no need. When a cup fell this way, it always split into halves. Neat.

So instead, she held the two halves in each palm to examine the break. The crack was a line, unnatural in its straightness. Something that existed solely as a mathematical concept. It was the day after In-chan's jesa.

It's better this way, she thought.

After all, if a bad thing had to happen, wasn't it better that it took place around the anniversary of some other awful thing? Some sort of assurance that this was the day when all awful things happened? There was, after all, an advantage to knowing. Jung-ha had read somewhere that Japanese death row inmates were not told about their date of execution. The logic being that their victims did not know when they died, so why should they? She used to think that it was poetic justice. But now, it felt like unnecessary cruelty. She'd want to know. Everyone deserved to know.

She gently ran her finger down the split and thought about pressing harder. She pictured her skin straining taut against the porcelain for a moment before it gave and parted with a gout of blood. The vertigo came, familiar and unbearable.

She put the pieces back down and swept her half-eaten breakfast into the garbage disposal.

"There's no point crying about it," she sternly told herself. "What's done is done."

The cup, after all, had fallen. A strange day would follow. This was the rule.

•

There was a time when Jung-ha's memory worked properly, a point in her life when she remembered and forgot like everyone else.

But something about what happened all those years ago, with In-chan, had perforated her brain. Holes opened up. Some were small and miniscule. Others yawning and wide as the dead black between the stars. And through them, her memories seeped out.

What she did remember was fixed, unmoving. What sank through that sieve, however, was gone for good. Court dates. Names of coworkers. Movies she watched a month ago. A year ago. She did not discriminate in what she lost.

"Where's the gochu-jeon," Mi-ri, Jung-ha's aunt, had said yesterday. She scrutinized the plates on the jesa table. "Wasn't that In-chan's favorite?"

"It's—" Jung-ha said as she looked around. Her shoulders sagged in disbelief. "I can't have forgotten it."

She had.

"Shit," she said. She pinched the bridge of her nose. "Shit, shit, shit."

Jung-ha looked at Mi-ri. She briefly wondered what her aunt

saw, what Jung-ha must've looked like to her. She wished for a mirror. What was the appropriate expression for this occasion? Apologetic? Sad?

She thought about explaining how In-chan had only really liked gochu-jeon because it was his father's favorite. She knew that it would just make things worse, but she wanted to explain anyway.

Mi-ri's face crumpled. For a moment, Jung-ha saw her mother there. Mi-ri struggled to rein in her emotions, the same way her sister used to. Her aunt turned and walked briskly toward her bag.

"Don't worry. I've brought some."

After the jesa, they moved the food to the kitchen counter and ate a rushed meal. Mi-ri picked up a piece of galbi with her chopsticks, considered it for a moment, and gingerly placed it over Jung-ha's bowl of rice. Jung-ha shook her head mutely.

"Still?" she asked, disappointed.

Jung-ha crammed some namul in her mouth in lieu of an answer. She chewed slowly. The food was cold, having sat out on the jesa table for over an hour. It tasted bland. Food offered to the dead could not be seasoned with anything besides salt. *Strong seasonings chase away spirits,* her mother had once told her. She wondered if their dead were so frail as to be kept at bay by minced garlic.

In-chan wouldn't want to be here, garlic or not, Jung-ha thought. The sesame oil made her lips slippery. She could feel a lump forming in her throat. She pushed it down with another spoonful of rice.

Before all this, back when Sang and Jung-ha were still married and she could still eat red meat—back when her lungs worked, and she used to make small talk with her coworkers—she and Sang used to watch documentaries.

Sang had picked the film that day. He nodded off almost immediately, but Jung-ha did not resent him for it. Ever since In-chan was born, Sang had worked double-time to pay the hospital bills.

The documentary was some small indie film about artisans and blacksmiths. Jung-ha had lost the rest of the film, but there was a scene that stuck. In a small workshop, a man restored a rusted cleaver until it shone. There was something beautiful in the way the cleaning solution ate away at the grime. Rust and steel—the two objects seemed one at first. Then they separated. She marveled at the way two things that seemed indistinguishable were made distinct.

Her memories were the same. Indistinguishable until time ate a part of it away to nothing. Whatever was left in her hands was sharp. Deadly.

◆

By the time she cleaned up the broken cup and set off to work, she was late. Jung-ha rushed into the classroom, late and wheezing. Her chest burned. She resented her ruined lungs, the sole witness to all that had occurred between her, her son, and her ex-husband.

The lecture was a bust. The muted sound of the cup shattering played over and over in her ears. From somewhere very far away, she heard her own voice as it droned on about postwar Modernist poets.

"Life is very long," it said. "Here we go round the prickly pear. Prickly pear prickly pear."

Her mother had raised prickly pears, back when Jung-ha was in middle school. She remembered them crowding the hallway. Between early spring and summer, little red flowers bloomed atop. It had amazed her, how such bright colors spilled out from the ugly muted green. When the flowers hardened into fruit, her mother tore the fleshy bulbs and made jam. It had stained their teeth red.

It was also in that narrow hallway that Jung-ha first heard a cup fall. Her hallway had always frightened her as a child. The intermittent lights from the windows turned most of it into a chiaroscuro. Lining the walls were shelves and frames, with the latter mostly consisting of dead ancestors and relatives. They gazed out into the darkness of the hallway, their printed eyes austere and unseeing. The shelves, on the other hand, were solely for her mother, who hoarded trophies, commemorations, and awards like a magpie.

Even now, she could recite the first few items in the hallway.

A very old and fragile-looking photograph (the sort that would've required a darkroom). Two second-place awards in a piano competition (awarded to one *Hwi Moon-hee*). A pressed and dried wedding bouquet (small and impressive). A black-and-white photograph of her grandfather (the one they used for his funeral). Another pressed and dried wedding bouquet (bigger this time).

That sudden sensation of falling, the kind that sometimes hit you on the verge of sleep, jolted her out of her daze. Jung-ha looked around to see that she had blanked out mid-lecture. From somewhere near the back, she heard a student scoff and leave.

"So sorry about that," she said. Her face burned with embarrassment. "Where was I?"

◆

She tried everything from grief counseling (expensive) to guided LSD trips (disastrous). But no matter what she did, she could not remember. She even resorted to a hypnotherapist. But after the session, he only shook his head apologetically.

"What," Jung-ha asked. "It didn't work?"

"I mean, that depends how you define *work*. You remembered a lot, but not what you actually wanted to remember."

He handed her one of those videocassettes and told her that it was a recording. She watched the video transcription exactly once, some few months after they had convicted Sang—after none of it mattered anymore. She had been temporarily staying with Mi-ri at the time.

Jung-ha got good and drunk and sat in her aunt's living room with the glow of her old TV filling her face.

"Where are you?" the man in the videotape asked.

"I'm in the kitchen."

"Who else is in the kitchen?"

"It's just me. In-chan's playing in his room."

"What are you doing?" asked the man, his voice soothing. "Are you cooking something?"

"I'm chopping meat. I'm making curry, I think."

"Where is In-chan now?"

From the TV screen, Jung-ha began to toss and turn.

"The cup," she mumbled. "The cup broke. But how did it fall? I didn't touch it."

"Jung-ha, I want you to focus. Do you remember locking the balcony door?"

"It always falls this way. Uninterrupted," Jung-ha said. "I'm trying to pick up the pieces."

"Jung-ha—"

"I think I've cut myself. It hurts."

"Jung-ha," the man asked. "Did you leave the balcony door open?"

"Ow. It hurts. Ow, ow, ow."

At some point, Jung-ha distantly realized that she was moaning. The grainy version of herself in the television was doing the same. Which one of the two had first started, she could not tell.

"The meat is so red," Jung-ha mumbled. "My fingers are too. It's all red. Bright ruby red."

Jung-ha never made it to the end of the videotape. She lurched to the toilet and threw up violently. From the living room, the videotape continued to play—the doctor's questions, never changing in pitch and tone, and hers, growing more and more incoherent.

Did you know that the balcony door was unlocked? Why didn't you close it? Did you know your son was going to fall?

Did you let him?

◆

At lunchtime, Jung-ha made a beeline for the corner of the teacher's lounge where she could sit undisturbed. Her stomach rumbled, but she had no appetite. There was a tap on her shoulders.

"How's it going, Jung-ha?" Joon asked.

Joon was the only one in the department who still talked to her on a regular basis. Jung-ha doubted it was out of genuine goodwill. At best, it was rubbernecking. More than likely, he was rubbing elbows with the hagwon's principal. They'd love to have any reason to fire her. She did not resent him for it. He was only doing what he felt like he needed to do, the same way everyone did.

"Hey, Joon," Jung-ha answered. "How are your lectures going?"

"Oh, you know. It's much of the same. There's a kid in my fourth period class—not sure what his deal is, exactly. A bit slow. Might be born with it? He's not autistic, I think. Maybe cerebral palsy? Sorry," he said, raising his hands in mocking placation. Jung-ha tried to remind herself that Joon only started working here a month ago, that he had no idea what had transpired. "I know we're supposed to tiptoe around this stuff—but all I'm saying is that you're wasting your money by enrolling this kid in a hagwon. Not to mention wasting my time and it disrupts the class."

Jung-ha took her lunch box and bashed Joon's head in with

it. She smashed his face with it until the stainless steel was sticky with spattered blood. Long after his feet stopped kicking, she mechanically lifted the lunch box and brought it down, over and over again.

"Jung-ha?" Joon asked, jostling her out of her daydream. "You still with us?"

"Hey, yeah, so sorry about that," she answered, eyes out of focus and wild. "I should get going. Have to eat lunch and prep for class."

"Oh, okay. What's on the menu today?"

"It's just some—"

Jung-ha tried to speak but was overcome by a fit of hacking. She hunched over, wheezing and coughing while Joon awkwardly averted his eyes.

After a moment, she spoke. "So sorry about that. Anyhow, it's just leftovers. In-chan's jesa was yesterday."

"Oh, I had no idea."

Joon stammered a useless apology before scurrying off. Jung-ha watched him go. Her hands shook.

◆

Lots of things changed after her husband tried to kill her, and then not much changed at all.

She gave up meat; her kidneys couldn't take it. The hagwon tried to fire her. Her presence made the parents gossip. She sued for wrongful termination and got them to settle. She refused their payout and instead asked for her job back.

Jung-ha continued to teach poetry from 8 to 12 and early American novels from 1 to 5. She still drove a Honda Odyssey. It was a family car, too big for her now. She kept it anyway.

•

The other documentary that Jung-ha really remembered was about some Russian filmmaker. His claim to fame was the idea that the same shot of an expressionless actor became something else when paired with different footage. A steaming bowl of soup. A woman stretched out on a divan. A dead child. The man magically became hungry or aroused or sad, depending on what came next. His point was that context meant everything. That when two things were put together, meaning was divined.

An egg breaking over a pan was breakfast. The same egg shattering against the floor was a waste. The fall in a rollercoaster was enjoyable because it was in the right context, a carefully crafted and monitored form of descent. Other falls were decidedly less pleasurable.

All those years ago, when Jung-ha first heard the quiet tinkling sound echoing around her mother's dark hallway, it took everything she had to not scream. Jung-ha had heard things break before; who hadn't? But the crack of the porcelain became something else in that hallway, in that tunnel where dead and forgotten things lurked on the walls.

When Jung-ha eventually found the courage to step forward,

she found what had been a teacup, just below a framed diploma. The cup looked expensive. She did not tell her mother—not then and not after what happened at school. Her ex-husband was the only person who ever heard this story.

"So, the cup sits on the shelf. It's jade green."

"Right."

"And there is no gust of wind. No tremor. It is so still that you could be convinced that the cup was a part of that shelf. And then the cup falls."

"Why?" Sang asked. "How?"

"It just does. Nothing propels it. It's on the shelf, until it isn't."

He looked skeptical, but his eyebrows were furrowed, and she could tell that he was absorbed by the story.

"Then it breaks?"

"No," she answered. "Break is the wrong word for it. It—"

She paused, searching for the right words.

"It comes apart. Two even halves."

"And you know that's how it happened?" he asked.

"Well, no. This is my imagination."

She told him the rest, how in her imagination the cup caught the light once as it tumbled end over end toward the floor. How it must've gleamed before it was bisected.

"Like a weary lighthouse."

"That's kind of beautiful," he said.

"Is it?" Jung-ha asked, taken aback. "I hadn't meant it that way."

"Yeah, I don't know. Almost sounded like you were describing something dying."

"Look who's waxing poetic now," she teased, laughing. She used to laugh like that back then, before all this.

He had been wrong, of course. But she did not know it back then. A person wasn't a teacup. A person did not come undone in the same way that a teacup did. The former was a chaotic and drawn-out affair. A hail of forms to sign and hushed whispers from your coworkers. It dragged out for years, long after one's child fell to his death off the balcony. The cup was eloquent, beautiful in its simplicity. There was a point where it was, beyond any doubt, a cup. And then it was not.

Did it become something else at that point? If Jung-ha had to guess, it was all context again. A shard of porcelain became a dagger in the wrong hands, with the wrong intentions. What was her intention? What was Sang's? Was there a point to knowing?

◆

After work, Jung-ha walked over to a restaurant for a meeting with concerned parents. They were probably just looking for a place to vent, disgruntled that the extracurricular classes had not adequately improved their children's test scores.

It was a Tuesday, but the restaurant was nearly full. Cubicle workers sat with their ties loosened, faces already red from soju. The parents were running late. A man sitting on the next table brayed with laughter, the sound piercing. A violent impulse throbbed.

Jung-ha wanted to do something insane, something horrible like taking the man's face and pressing it into the grill. She wanted to do something that wouldn't help anyone or anything—in fact, she wanted to do something that would make everything worse. *Is this how Sang felt?* she wondered.

·

There was a second part to the cup story, one that she kept to herself. Partially because no one would believe her. It also felt too private. It revealed too much, although what it revealed exactly, she did not know.

That day, when the cup fell for the very first time, her school had served dead birds for lunch. There was an odd silence in the cafeteria. Utensils quietly clicked against the plastic trays. Jung-ha diligently waited in line, staring at the back of another student's head.

Behind the lunch counter was a worker Jung-ha had never seen. There was a redness to his face that she associated with sunburns and aging drunks who ranted and raved in the subways. His hand was equally ruddy. He motioned her closer, and she skittishly stuck out her lunch tray.

He smiled as he ladled a spoonful of meat over the rice. Something about the way the meat fluidly slid over the rice was haunting.

"Do you know what this is?" he asked.

She shook her head. Her throat felt very small.

"Flesh."

It was her second year of international school; her English

wasn't all that good. But even still, that word sounded off to her.

"Excuse me?" she asked. "I don't think I heard—"

"The flesh of a dead bird," he answered.

She wanted to ask further, but a teacher came and ushered her along. Even after sitting down, she could feel the man's gaze, intent and wild. His lips were rapidly twitching, mouthing the same word again and again.

Eat. Eat. Eat. Eat. Eat eaaaaaaaaat eateateateateateateateateat.

Sensing her hesitation, his face twisted into a grimace of anger. He began to walk toward her, his gait strange and stilted. It reminded Jung-ha of pigeons, the way they dragged their bloated bodies to peck at scraps. She hurriedly began shoving forkfuls into her mouth, afraid of what the man might do. The meat was stringy and overcooked. Jung-ha's stomach churned.

Twenty minutes later, she was kneeling in a toilet cubicle and retching her guts out. Amidst her heaving, she heard the bathroom door open.

"You're throwing it up, aren't you?" a voice asked. "That bird gave up its flight for you."

What does that even mean, Jung-ha wanted to ask. But violent vertigo seized her again; she puked some more instead. A thunderous slam rocked the cubicle. She realized with a start of terror that the man was beating his fists against the thin wall of the cubicle.

"Do you fucking hear me," he shouted. "That bird became

undone for you."

The man was having trouble speaking, it seemed, rage rendering his words unintelligible. Strange squawking noises punctuated his speech. Jung-ha buried her head between her knees and screamed. The last thing she saw was a large pair of avian feet desperately clawing at the gap between the floor and the cubicle. But when the teachers eventually found her, she was unconscious and alone in the bathroom.

Later, she retraced her steps in her mother's hallway. She aimed her flashlight at a shelf to see that the cup was missing. The pieces, likewise, were gone.

What cup? was the only thing her mother said when Jung-ha asked about it.

◆

The parents eventually arrived. Three mothers and a father. They sat in a circle around the dinner table and picked at the food.

"So, Ms. Hwi," one of them, the clear leader of the group, spoke. "We don't mean to be overbearing."

But you are about to be anyway, Jung-ha thought.

"Some of the other parents have said that there is a student with, well, I'm not sure what's the right way to say this, but they have a condition?"

Jung-ha's heart sank. From somewhere deep down, the same old anger stirred, but she was tired now.

"Cerebral palsy," Jung-ha answered dully. "Affects about two to three children out of a thousand."

It surprised her that she still remembered the statistics.

"Yes, okay, so you are aware," the parent answered.

Relief washed over her face and Jung-ha hated her for it. She wanted to grab the parent by the collar and shake her. *What the hell do you know,* she wanted to scream. And then the floor dropped out of her anger. Guilt clenched her throat shut and whispered in her ears.

Like you didn't cry when you first found out about how your son was born, it said. *Like you never looked at other kids with envy or got the monthly medical bill and resented him for it.*

Jung-ha neither screamed nor shouted. She stared at her plate instead. The fish stared back, its opaque, dead eyes looking into nothing.

·

Jung-ha was in getting her PhD when the cup fell into halves for the second time. That was the same day her mother stopped answering her texts.

Two days later, Jung-ha took a train back home. She opened the door to find everything was in its place, save for some of her mother's clothes, jewelry, and books. On the tear-off calendar, she found a scrawled note. It explained everything and nothing at once. Jung-ha never heard from her mother again, the first vanishing of many.

·

After the parents' meeting, Jung-ha drove in a daze. She thought of birds and cups. A small, terrified figure flailing its arms as it plummeted toward the ground. There was a wet thud against the windshield and Jung-ha screamed and wrenched the steering wheel. The vehicle crossed into the pedestrian walkway, narrowly missed a passerby, and crashed into the railing. On the windshield was something that had once been a bird.

"What the fuck," the person screamed. "What the hell is wrong with you?"

"I'm sorry," Jung-ha whispered, over and over again. "I'm so sorry."

Before she could get out of the car, another bird plummeted into it, then another. In no time, the falling birds beat a thrumming tattoo, flesh tearing against glass and steel. Jung-ha began to laugh. Quietly at first, then louder and louder until she doubled up and pounded her fist into the driving wheel. Fat teardrops of mirth ran down her face.

"What's happening?" the man stammered. "Why are you *laughing*?"

"I spent," she said, laughing and wheezing, "the entire day so terrified of what would happen. So afraid. When a cup falls that way, strange things always happen."

Birds crashed themselves around her. She could barely hear herself over the thundering rain of feather and beak. The man backed away from Jung-ha's car, then began running away in earnest.

"And here it is, the strange event," she sang to herself. "So why the disappointment?"

Maybe a part of her had looked forward to something strange happening. Something that wasn't this, this monotonous aftermath her entire life had become.

By the time the rain of birds petered out, the angry pedestrian was a distant dot. She got out of the car, sidestepping the dead birds. She sat on the edge of the bridge with her legs dangling through the railing. One of her shoes fell off, the dark water of the river below swallowing it in moments. With a shrug, she took off her other shoe and lobbed it over the railing.

.

Whether it had been guilt, frayed nerves, or a change of heart, Jung-ha had no way of knowing. All she knew was that Sang had confessed to what he did almost immediately. It was what saved her life.

By the time EMS arrived, she had nearly choked to death on her own vomit. What came out of her mouth was an oily shade of blue and stank to high hell. It was later that Jung-ha learned the medical slang for someone who came in with Gramoxone poisoning was a Smurf, on account of the blue coloration of their skin and vomit.

You did what you thought you had to do, was the last thing Sang had ever said to her. *I did what I thought I had to do.*

It was touch-and-go for several days, but she pulled through. She didn't remember much of those few days. Despite everything, at least when it came to this, she was grateful that her memory had failed her. Later, a harried-looking doctor walked in to inform Jung-ha that her lungs and kidneys would never really recover.

"A teaspoon of this stuff is enough to kill most people," he said. "Frankly, it's a miracle that you survived at all."

She lay in her hospital bed and took his words in. A machine beeped overhead. The tube in her mouth tasted of plastic.

On the day she was discharged from the hospital, a nurse congratulated her.

"You should be grateful," he told her.

By the time security peeled Jung-ha off him, Jung-ha had fractured the nurse's jaw. She looked down at her knuckles and marveled at the way they swelled, and at her own capacity for violence.

◆

"Hello?" her aunt Mi-ri answered. "Jung-ha?"

"I crashed the car."

"Oh my god. Do you need help?"

"It's fine. I called insurance."

There was a pause, then Jung-ha spoke again. "Why do you think that Sang did that?"

There was a shocked silence over the phone.

"Jung-ha?" Mi-ri asked.

"Sang. He said he did what he had to do, as did I."

"Jung-ha," Mi-ri said again.

"Maybe he thought I—" Jung-ha's voice broke. She could not bring herself to say it. She laughed, and the sound was wet and wheezy. "I mean, we couldn't afford In-chan's hospital bills, that much was true. Maybe I wanted that to happen. Maybe I let him wander to the balcony, knowing that it was unlocked."

"Jung-ha, listen."

"No, imo, you listen. After everything that's happened, after In-chan, after Sang, the poisoning—*everything*. My only real regret is that I looked down."

The desire to gag and cough wrestled for control over Jung-ha's body. She grit her teeth, denying both.

"I can't remember In-chan's face anymore."

A silence ensued. Just when she began to wonder if Mi-ri had hung up, her aunt spoke.

"When we were both children, our father had a factory."

She paused as if waiting for an answer.

"I didn't know," Jung-ha said.

"It was a textile factory that his father built shortly after we got our independence back."

There was another pause, longer this time.

"Sometimes, your mother and I said the factory was his real child, " she said. "He'd go out to that factory at the crack of dawn and come back, stinking of all the ink that they used to dye the textile."

"Imo, where are you going with this?"

"It burned," she said. "All of it. Down to the ground. It destroyed him. He took to drinking afterward, and then the divorce came not long after that."

Mi-ri sighed.

"Last we heard, he was working in construction to make ends meet and they dropped a concrete pillar on him. Gone like that. Not even enough left to bury."

There was another long pause.

"Actually," Mi-ri said, "I burned that factory to the ground."

"It was November," she said. "We used to smoke behind the factory, your mother and me. I remember the sky being so blue, the kind that makes you a little dizzy to look up. Windy day too. Perfect for a fire."

"Imo, you couldn't have known."

"No, it's okay. I feel better thinking that way, to think that I burned it all down. It's a weight off, I think."

"What do you mean?"

"I mean, I beat the hell out of myself over it for years. I'd think to myself, 'Mi-ri, why didn't you just make sure that cigarette was out? Why couldn't you just have looked twice?'"

The sun had now set. The river below was a strange, malignant growth, some twisting parasite that had attached itself to the city.

"But the alternative seemed worse. To think that all this awful happened out of sheer chance. That there was no reason for any of this to happen. That was too much, you know?"

◆

Insurance came. They offered a ride back home but Jung-ha turned it down. She instead got up and began to walk toward the end of the bridge, still barefoot.

"Hey," one of the insurance workers called out after her. "Are you alright?"

She waved without looking and walked. It was a part of the city that Jung-ha had never been to, but she kept walking. Her lungs gave out long before her feet did, and she breathlessly sat at a bus station. She got onto the first bus that arrived. She did not check the route; she didn't ask the driver where it was going either. It didn't matter. It had to stop somewhere.

SEPARATION ANXIETY

"Look alive, boss, we're loading," Hyeok-gi shouted.

"Which ones?"

"The whelps. Aisles two to four. I've marked the ones that are shipping out."

Gwi scanned the aisles. Some sixty or so cages, too many for Hyeok-gi to load on his own. He sighed. Morning would consist entirely of work, it seemed. The trucker did not leave his vehicle, and rolled up the window shortly after being paid. Gwi did not blame him. The dog factory smelled. It wasn't an outright stench, exactly.

He ran a clean shop as far as dog mills went. Back when he was just the hired help, the owner didn't even bother cleaning out the urine and feces. When the dogs in the upper cages pissed, it just flowed down to the lower dogs. It was the first thing Gwi changed after buying the place.

But hundreds of bodies were crammed into the cages. What would have been fine on its own, when scaled up like this, coalesced into something else. There was too much life in too small a space. And it was this muchness that caused the smell. It was impossible, Gwi learned, for life to be odorless.

Sweat and saliva. The gunk that built up in the corner of the dogs' eyes. The legs of the smaller dogs often sank through the wire cages, scraping them raw over time. Blood hardened to scabs or boiled over to pus. And it all smelled.

No matter how often they hosed down the cages, those tiny bits of life accumulated—in the creases of his shirts, on his already thinning hairline, beneath his fingernails. After work, he'd wrangle off his sweat-soaked shirt and imagine an invisible cloud of powdered dog exploding out of him. He took it in when he breathed, turned it into a part of him.

Too many dogs in his lungs. That was what the previous owner used to say whenever a part-timer burned out and quit.

His phone buzzed. It was a text.

Hey, I know it's been a while, but I . . .

The rest was hidden, lumped into ellipses. When Gwi read that the text was from Ee-oon, he froze, his face illuminated by the pale glow of the screen. There was another message.

Only if you're okay with it, that is.

When Gwi got home, he lay in the dark and wondered what it was that he could be okay with. He wondered if the word *okay* would ever be applicable to Ee-oon and him. He bolted up and did something he hadn't done in years: he pictured coming clean to Ee-oon, then thought of all the things he might say in response. In many of those imagined scenarios, Ee-oon was crying. In others, he shouted and raved, spittle flying from his mouth.

Once, this had been a daily ritual, something that Gwi started not long after Ee-oon moved away. There was a time when these imagined accusations were more of a dance, rather than a conversation: Gwi turning his answers and excuses over and over again until they were as smooth and well-worn as the inside of a ring.

Why? the Ee-oon in his mind asked.

His undershirt felt too small. From somewhere outside, a dog began to bark. There was one at first, then two, and then too many to count. Gwi buried his head under the pillow. But the sound was everywhere, its distance indeterminable.

They had both been fourteen when they met. Gangly, awkward

things that were still growing into their bodies.

Gwi had known him as the new kid in town and not much else. When Gwi first saw him, the boy was in the middle of stealing books from the library.

"I think you need to check those out," Gwi had said.

The other boy shrugged instead of answering. He continued to sweep armfuls of books off the shelf. They fell with a resounding clatter, but no one came to examine the noise. The boy got on his knees and scoured through the pile, eventually selecting one more book. It had a butterfly on the cover, although Gwi could not remember what the name of the book was. The other boy got up, dusted his knees, and began walking toward another shelf.

"Hey, hold on," Gwi snapped.

He grabbed the other boy by the wrist, pulling his arm away from the shelves. The boy's wiry frame lifted along with his arm. His skin was pale. In the middle of it were a pair of perfect black circles. Gwi thought of dice. It took a few moments for it to sink in; they were bruises.

"Hey," Gwi said again, less angry and more bemused now.

That was as far as Gwi got. The book thief wound his arm and punched him, right on his nose. The boy was small, but he did not hold back. It was enough to send Gwi's head reeling. His nose sang with dull pain. He watched as the boy shrugged and sauntered away.

Gwi chased him down the emergency stairwell, but he could

not pick up speed, afraid that his momentum would send him tumbling end over end. No such fear seemed to inhibit the other boy. He skipped over four to five stairs at a time, barely sticking the landing each time.

Gwi stumbled out of the stairwell, his lungs burning. He looked up just in time to see the double doors of the main entrance swing open and shut, the other boy bolting through. The boy briefly turned and flashed Gwi a smile. There was something striking to it that made Gwi stop in his tracks. He stood, rooted in place, as the thief rapidly dwindled to a dot beyond it.

Gwi liked and pitied his dogs. They were frail things, easy to impress. All of them were fed kibble, but Gwi would sometimes give them bits of his food. Not all of them of course, just the ones he liked. It was mere scraps, but enough to win their loyalty. Those dogs, the ones he fed personally, trailed him whenever they were let out of the cages.

Something about the new batch of dogs, however, irked him. He had made the purchase on recommendation.

"Purebreds are where the real money is," the man had told him.

"I already have purebreds," Gwi answered mechanically.

"No, no. I'm talking about the real deal. Not the half mutts used to gouge chumps. I'm talking pedigree."

And so, the new dogs were shipped in. These dogs were different. They required special attention, specific kinds of feed.

"Not just kibble. They need supplements and vitamins," said the truck driver that brought the dogs.

Gwi laughed. Surely, he was joking. The man did not laugh back.

"No cages either," he said before driving off.

He followed all the instructions, down to the letter. He instructed Hyeok-gi, the part-timer, to carefully feed and brush the dogs. He allowed them to stay inside the shipping container he'd turned into an office space.

The office, if the repurposed container could be called that, was sparse. There was a mini fridge, two desks, and a beat-up fan. There used to be a folding cot, but he put it in storage for the pure-breds.

Hyeok-gi had already clocked out. Gwi rummaged around the mini fridge for a beer. One of the purebreds pawed at its expensive kennel. It was no longer a pup, but not quite fully grown either. It would not be another month or so before it became mature enough to breed.

Gwi stuck a finger through a hole in the kennel and scratched the dog's head. But the dog, no longer a pup, let out a snarl and nipped at his finger. Not hard enough to hurt him, but enough to anger him.

"Knock it off," he shouted.

The animal flinched and Gwi felt an immediate twinge of guilt.

"Sorry," he told the dog and resumed scratching its head. "But you know, you have it lucky. You have no idea what the other dog farms are like."

Gwi had seen dogs being forced to give birth until their bodies simply gave out. It usually took around fifty pups. Gwi even once heard a man boast about how he cut a dog's belly open.

"She was pregnant with eight pups when she keeled," the man had said. "I wasn't going to let that go to waste."

Gwi shook his head in disgust at the memory. He looked down at the small dog.

"Enjoy it while you can. Trust me, it doesn't get much better than this."

Gwi was in the middle of feeding the rejects when his phone rang.

"Hello?" a man asked. "Is this Gwi?"

"Yes, who is this?"

"Gwi." The voice laughed. "It's me. Ee-oon."

He clutched at the bag of feed, feeling it slip out of his fingers. He distantly heard it hit the floor and burst open, its contents spilling out. A frenzy went up among the cages. Snouts pressed against walls and claws caught on wires. The rejects were unlike the rest of the dogs. Abandoned and half-feral, they were sold off to Gwi for pennies on the dollar. The relatively good-looking ones became breeding stock. The rest were loaded onto a truck and sold at the marketplace. It was the one reason he needed Hyeok-gi. Gwi could not bear to watch them be loaded up. Nothing good awaited those dogs. Most vanished into roiling pots of broth and spices.

"Hello? Are you there?" asked Ee-oon. "I'm sorry, should I call back?"

"No, no," Gwi said. "It's fine."

They talked for a while like that. Ee-oon asked a lot of questions about the town. Was the coffee shop still there? ("Burned down a couple years back.") Was the vinyl shop still run by the same man? ("He still blames me for those vinyl records you stole.")

"Do you remember that time when we ditched class and hitchhiked to go see the ocean?" Ee-oon asked.

"Yeah," Gwi answered, then laughed. He had forgotten all about it until Ee-oon brought it up. "I'm amazed that we got away with skipping class at all—I didn't even think we were going to make it to the ocean."

A lapse fell in their conversation. Gwi wanted to pick it up, but he could not think of anything to say.

"Anyhow," Ee-oon said after a while. "What I really wanted to ask was—"

Gwi felt his stomach twist. He pressed the phone harder against his ear, the way one applied a tourniquet to a wound.

"Sorry, what was that? I couldn't quite catch it."

"Well, like my text said, I'm going to be visiting for a week or so. I was just wondering if I could crash?"

"Oh."

"Sorry, I know this is all very out of the blue."

"No, it's fine, not a problem at all."

He told Gwi that he would arrive on Tuesday. They agreed to meet at the oxtail restaurant.

"Okay, well, great," Ee-oon said. "I'll see you then?"

"Wait."

"What is it?"

"Never mind. It's good to hear from you again."

"Oh. Yeah, me too." A pause. "Thanks, Gwi."

The line went dead. Gwi filled the dog bowls, feeling strangely defeated.

Once, back when Gwi was still learning how to be a dog farmer, his boss at the time told him to get rid of dead dogs.

"Get this out of here," he said, pointing toward a small pile of dog carcasses. Gwi drove to the supermarket and bought a trash bag, one of those giant hundred-liter bags marked *Municipal Solid Waste*. He filled it to the brim with dead dogs, not realizing how heavy it would become. Sweat poured down his back.

Gwi had lugged the trash bag halfway out of the factory when he felt a sharp crack at the back of his head. It was his boss.

"What the fuck are you doing?" he had asked. "You're going to just lug that to the garbage pin and then what—leave it there for the trucks to pick it up? Are you trying to advertise that there's a dog farm here?"

"Well, what the hell do you want me to do with this?"

"Take it up to the woods and throw it down the ravine," he said. "Where no one will find it."

The bag made a sickening crunch when Gwi threw it away, a sound that haunted him to this day. The first thing that Gwi bought for his dog farm was an industrial-sized incinerator.

Ee-oon was already there when Gwi walked into the restaurant. His posture radiated ease, as if he had never left. The owner of the restaurant stood across from him and laughed at some joke he made.

Gwi wavered, unable to decide if he wanted to greet his friend or bolt out of the building. Before Gwi could decide, Ee-oon spotted him and flashed him that particular smile of his.

They drank while waiting for their food to come out. Gwi asked about Ee-oon's life in Seoul, but his answers were vague, bordering on evasive.

"But enough about me," Ee-oon said. "Honestly? I missed this."

Ee-oon gestured at the restaurant. It comforted Gwi somehow, to know that he and his town weren't things that Ee-oon discarded entirely.

And yet the fact of it was plain; his town was on its way out. The population dwindled with each year that passed. Most left for bigger cities; few ever returned. Those who did joylessly breezed through their old haunts. Some of them unfortunately remembered Gwi, which meant that he had to stop for a minute or two and chat. They invariably praised how different the metropolis was. Either that, or they left backhanded compliments—marveling at every minor retail chain that set up shop in Gwi's town.

"Wow, we have a CGV theater?" Gwi remembered one of them asking. "When did we get that?"

We. Gwi resented that pronoun, how it assumed kinship. The truth was that they were visiting to remind themselves that what they left behind wasn't much. But Ee-oon seemed different. He did not want to talk about his life in Seoul, instead insisting on hounding Gwi about every little thing that happened while he was gone—things about the town and how their mutual friends were doing. Despite everything, Gwi found himself smiling.

"What's that like, working with all those dogs?" Ee-oon asked.

Gwi felt his smile falter. His job paid well, to be sure. But it wasn't glamorous work.

"It's good," he said, then joked. "It's noisy. I'll tell you that much."

"I heard that there are some dog factories with awful conditions."

"Yeah, but mine isn't like that," Gwi answered, suddenly severe. "You can come and look around."

"No, I wasn't implying that you were running your place like that," Ee-oon said, raising a placating hand.

"Yeah, but I'm serious."

The food arrived. Ee-oon dug around his steaming bowl for a bit, fished out a large oxtail, and dropped it into Gwi's soup.

"Here," he said.

"What, you still don't eat oxtail?" Gwi asked, digging his fingers into the little nooks of the bone to dig out the meat.

"It's not for me."

"You should've told me," Gwi teased. "I think I saw a nice chicken nugget and fries on the kid's menu section."

"Haha, very funny," Ee-oon said. He flicked a piece of rice at Gwi. "I just don't like eating things off the bone."

Ee-oon spooned a mouthful, then made an appreciative noise.

"Yeah, I missed this," he said.

Gwi looked around the restaurant. Taped to the walls were grainy photos, depicting the time some TV show introduced the restaurant as a hidden gem. That had been well over ten years ago. The customers at the restaurant were either old or quickly getting there. Gwi and Ee-oon were some of the youngest in the place. What was it that Ee-oon had missed? Gwi wondered.

"What brought you back?"

The question had slipped out before Gwi could help it. It was, of course, not the question he wanted to ask, the one that went *Do you know what I did?* But there was no way he could ever ask that question. Even in his imaginary scenarios, where Ee-oon screamed and wept, the conversation began with Ee-oon somehow finding out. Just the thought of asking the question himself made Gwi nauseous.

Gwi could not lift his eyes up from the bowl of soup. He heard Ee-oon take a breath and almost flinched; he felt like one of his dogs.

"My father passed away earlier this year. Turns out our old house was still under his deed. I'm just getting that sorted."`

His voice sounded tired, but normal otherwise. Gwi thought of his friend's father. More nausea coiled inside him, this time tinged with that old, righteous anger. Ee-oon's father had been a piece of shit.

When they got back home, Gwi insisted that Ee-oon take the bed. Ee-oon weakly protested, too weary from the alcohol and the journey to say no. Gwi lay on the air mattress on the floor. His house looked strange and unfamiliar from this new vantage point. A world as seen by one of his dogs.

"Hey," Gwi said. "Why don't you like eating oxtail?"

"I just don't like what it's attached to."

Gwi didn't understand what he meant, but he didn't ask any further. Ee-oon was quiet for a while. Just as Gwi was about to give up and sleep, Ee-oon spoke.

"Meat and bone. Something horrible about the way they separate."

It had been a month later, when school started, that Gwi saw Ee-oon for the second time. His seat ended up being next to his.

"Hey, I know you," Ee-oon said brightly. Gwi stared at him, at a loss, then ignored him pointedly.

"What are you reading?" Ee-oon asked, unbothered.

Gwi did not answer, turning his back again.

"*Gulliver's Travels*," said Ee-oon, making Gwi turn again. "I liked that book too."

They became friends, in that way kids in proximity often did. Soon, Gwi came to realize that Ee-oon stole all sorts of things. But his favorite marks were books—or really anything printed on paper that fit into his worn and gray JanSport. He did not care what books he stole. Service manuals. Hymnals. Airplane safety instructions. Funeral service brochures. He rarely got caught. It wasn't because he was some master thief. Rather, it was the effortless lack of concern that accompanied his theft, the kind of sheer nonchalance that made the universe throw its hands up in rueful admiration. Ee-oon did not fit in with Gwi's little town. He was an other, something foreign. He did not have many friends but always got top marks.

Ee-oon's family had moved down to this small city, all the way from Seoul. People exchanged rumors, speculating as to why a man and his son suddenly moved here—with mother nowhere to be seen. Some claimed that Ee-oon's father was a once-famous professor who fled scandal after getting involved with a student. Others claimed that the father was part of a Ponzi scheme in hiding from the authorities. No one knew for sure. What was true, however, was that Ee-oon was interesting. And Ee-oon's friendship with Gwi, by proxy, also made Gwi interesting.

Ee-oon was busy the next day. He had meetings with lawyers and realtors over the matter of his father's house. Gwi did not complain.

I have my own work, Gwi thought to himself. *I've got things to do.*

He dragged a chair out of the office, one of those stackable plastic ones. The legs of the chair kicked up dust as it scraped against the ground. He placed the chair in the middle of the factory and sat there, surrounded by a wall of cages.

Gwi peered at the dogs and thought of the time when he first saw Ee-oon's father. He had never believed in any of the rumors. Gwi didn't need to resort to gossip; he, out of everyone in the town, knew Ee-oon.

He alone knew that Ee-oon's family was not well off. Gwi had seen the stacks of envelopes in Ee-oon's mailbox. Some were labeled *Basic Livelihood Security Services* while others were notices for unpaid bills. He didn't say anything to anybody, of course. He was better than that.

Gwi also knew that Ee-oon did not steal books out of need; when Gwi first visited Ee-oon's house, he saw that the walls were lined with bookshelves, nearly all of them full.

"I heard that you were a good friend to my son," Ee-oon's father had said. "Will you be staying for dinner?"

"We're just here to study for a bit," Ee-oon had said, cutting his father off. "Gwi won't be staying."

It had shocked Gwi, the dull timbre of his friend's voice. The house had been clean, but the furniture and appliances were in bad shape. The fridge was a relic from another time, the sort with a latch instead of magnetic doors. From time to time, it let loose an unearthly roar that made Gwi jump. They sat quietly in the kitchen and did their homework. They had worked in silence; there was something austere about the house that invited quiet.

Gwi remembered noticing a sound, almost imperceptible at first, then growing louder and louder. Eventually, Gwi had to put his textbooks down.

"What is that noise," he had whispered.

"I have to study," Ee-oon had answered, in that same quiet, dead voice.

From his seat, he could just barely see the living room. Ee-oon's father was sitting on the couch, reading the papers. The man's left hand held a pair of acupressure balls, those heavy metal spheres that left little tracks of red pressure marks on the man's weathered hand. He looked back at Ee-oon and thought that he saw his friend's shoulder quiver. Gwi thought of his pale skin and those neat concentric circles of blue-black bruises.

A high, yipping scream startled Gwi from his thoughts. He cursed, spilling his beer. One of the dogs had sunk its fangs into the other dog's back. Little flecks of blood stained the white teeth. Gwi got up, slowly walked toward the cage with the fighting dogs, and pried them apart with his feet.

"Knock it off," he said. "You'll miss seeing other dogs when you're gone, sold off to some snot-nosed brat that'll pull your ears and step on your tails."

Gwi sat back down but stood up almost immediately. He paced around the facility, suddenly restless. He idly ran his fingers along the cages as he walked, his fingers hitting the wires with a dull ringing noise. Some of the dogs flinched at the sound, which annoyed Gwi. He grabbed a bag of dried squid legs from the office and threw bits of it at the dogs.

"I'm your friend, you idiots," he muttered as he watched the small mounds of fur wrestle each other for the scraps of food.

I'm free after six, read Ee-oon's text. *Let's grab a drink.*

Where did you have in mind? Gwi typed before he realized his mistake. Many of the bars and restaurants had shut down over the years, with very few cropping up to take their place. Gwi erased the text and instead sent him the address to a taproom, one of those franchises that never really impressed but didn't disappoint either. Once inside, Gwi wanted to sit at a table by the corner, but Ee-oon insisted on the bar.

"So," Gwi asked. "Did you get everything sorted?"

"Yeah," he said. "It was a hassle, but it's done."

It was a Wednesday, but as time passed, the bar began to fill. Ee-oon began striking up conversations with anyone he recognized.

"Seongju High?" he'd say. "I was in Class One? I think you were in Class Two."

Most did not remember who he was, which was better than the alternative. Gwi could see the dismay on the faces of those that did remember Ee-oon. It was brief, and quickly smoothed over, but there regardless.

Can he not see it? Gwi wondered. *Or does he just not mind.*

He studied Ee-oon's face but could not tell what he was thinking. Still, Ee-oon quickly managed to gather a small crowd of people, most of them former classmates. They chewed the fat together and laughed, while Gwi sipped his beer and became more and more inexplicably upset. Their conversation became droning white noise that Gwi pushed to the back of his mind, the same way he did with his dogs barking.

"Remember that?" Ee-oon asked him suddenly. Gwi blinked as everyone turned their heads toward him.

"Oh yeah, that was funny," Gwi answered. He could tell by the confusion in Ee-oon's face that it was the wrong answer.

"Sorry, I have to use the washroom," Gwi said as he stood abruptly.

Like Ee-oon's poverty and theft, Gwi kept quiet about Ee-oon's father as well. As he had left Ee-oon's house that day, something about Gwi's face must have given him away—Ee-oon stared at him for a bit, shook his head, then simply said:

"Don't."

Don't do what? And why? Gwi's head was full of questions. Why did Ee-oon steal all those books? Why did Ee-oon's father treat Ee-oon that way?

Gwi figured out some things on his own. He realized that Ee-oon's decisions to wear long sleeves coincided with the days graded tests or report cards came out. Gwi cherished the other questions, even the unanswered ones. They were questions that only he and Ee-oon shared. Ee-oon had not seen fit to tell anyone else, not even when the history teacher asked Ee-oon to stay after class.

"Not you, Gwi," the teacher said. "Just Ee-oon."

But Gwi did not leave. He instead waited outside the classroom with his ear to the wooden sliding doors.

". . . and you have nothing to tell me?"

Gwi pressed harder against the door, but he could not make out what Ee-oon was saying. He stood like that for what seemed ages—his teacher's questions growing in volume and concern, punctuated by a quiet whisper from Ee-oon.

The door slid open. Gwi looked up to see Ee-oon, his friend's expression unreadable. Gwi tried to apologize, but something else slipped out.

"Did you tell him?"

Ee-oon opened his mouth, closed it, then mutely shook his head. He pushed past Gwi and walked down the hallway. Gwi watched him go. A heavy, sticky feeling settled in his guts. Relief and acute shame, all mixed up and jumbled until they became impossible to separate.

◆

They left the bar around midnight. Ee-oon had wanted to stay but Gwi insisted on leaving, citing work. It was September, but the nights were already cold. Gwi walked briskly, shivering in his thin jacket. He eventually noticed that he could not hear Ee-oon's footsteps. He turned to see Ee-oon standing at the far end of the alleyway, rooted to the spot.

"What are you doing?" Gwi said, quietly at first, then louder. "Ee-oon! What are you doing?"

Ee-oon did not move. Cursing under his breath, Gwi walked back the way he came.

"Hey, Ee-oon." Gwi shook his shoulders. "Come on, it's freezing."

Ee-oon wordlessly gestured at the house in front of him. Gwi looked up to see the outline of a familiar house. The two of them stood in the dark like that for a while.

"It wasn't much," Ee-oon said quietly. "But it used to be home."

Gwi shivered, although he could no longer tell if it was because of the cold. He tried to make out Ee-oon's expression, but it was too dark. He stared at that indistinct lump that was Ee-oon's face.

"Yeah, well, not anymore."

As the college applications neared, the frequency of the bruises increased. Gwi watched, anguished, as Ee-oon retreated further into himself. Finally, one day, while lobbing rocks together off a bridge, Gwi spoke up.

"He can't keep this up," he said. "And neither can you."

Ee-oon said nothing and chucked another rock, squinting against the sun to see where it landed.

"I mean it," Gwi said.

"It's fine," Ee-oon said. "I'm applying to other colleges besides the one my father wants. If I get a full-ride, I can put all of this behind me."

Gwi blinked.

"Other colleges?" he asked. "I thought you were just applying to those four schools that we talked about."

Although he had not told Ee-oon, Gwi had also applied to the same four places. Ee-oon had never asked Gwi where he was applying, which stung—in a way that he could not exactly place.

"No," Ee-oon answered. His back was turned to Gwi. That upset him. Why wouldn't he look at Gwi? And why had Ee-oon not told him this? Did they not share everything?

"That's just to keep my father off my back," Ee-oon continued to speak. "I don't want to go to any of those places."

Gwi found his eyes tearing inexplicably. He wiped his eyes angrily.

"Where?" he demanded. Ee-oon lobbed another rock instead, still refusing to look at Gwi. "Where?"

The word came as a shout now, and Ee-oon at last turned to glance at him. Gwi expected to see shame, or even guilt. Why hadn't Ee-oon told him?

"Where?"

"Who cares," Ee-oon answered, lobbing more rocks. "Anywhere is good, as long as it's not this."

Ee-oon swept his arm in a circle to gesture at all the things around him. Gwi licked his lips, his mouth suddenly parched. Something venomous arose within him, unnamed and ugly.

They brought out folding chairs to watch the sunset. The sunlight refracted off the rows of stainless-steel cages.

"You ever feel lucky while you work?" Ee-oon asked, staring at the field of quietly heaving bodies.

"Feel lucky about what? Getting bitten every other day?"

"To be surrounded by all these things that can't go anywhere, knowing that you can."

"What's that supposed to mean," Gwi said, hating the way his voice quivered.

"I sometimes have the feeling that you like it."

Gwi tried to stand but couldn't. His limbs felt ethereal and disconnected. Still, Ee-oon continued to speak and stare at the dogs.

"To look at caged things."

Gwi tried to make a sound, but no sound escaped his lips. Ee-oon's face began to elongate, stretching like the muzzle of a dog. Ee-oon turned his head and grinned. A very long, pink tongue rolled out of his mouth. Saliva and hot, stinking air poured out of his open mouth.

"Selfish," Ee-oon said. Words dribbled out of his misshapen jaw, mangled and barely comprehensible. "Too cowardly to leave but too selfish to let others go."

Saying so, he stretched his mouth open impossibly wide and bit down on Gwi's head.

Gwi jerked awake with a short cry, his sweat leaving a dark stain on the air mattress.

A week or two after the conversation at the bridge, Gwi had run into Ee-oon's father.

"How are your applications going?" he asked Gwi. "How's Ee-oon?"

That was when Gwi let slip about Ee-oon's applications, how he planned to move far away. He hadn't meant anything by it. No, that wasn't true. Maybe he had, but what was wrong with letting a father know about his son's plans? No, untrue again. Gwi had known that it was wrong, that what he had done was unforgivable, that there would be consequences.

Why had Gwi done that? What was so important about Ee-oon that simply the thought of him up and vanishing one day twisted his insides this way, made his guts writhe and churn until all those words tumbled out of his mouth? He didn't know—no, that was wrong yet again. He didn't want to know.

•

Gwi wanted to make a big deal out of Ee-oon's final night, but his friend insisted on sitting on the park bench and drinking.

"So, once all this is taken care of, what are you going to do?" Gwi asked.

"What do you mean?"

"You know, are you going back up to the city?"

"Yeah, I should get going."

"What's it like?"

"It's not all that it's chalked up to be, trust me," Ee-oon said.

"I mean, that doesn't tell me much. What makes you want to go back?"

Ee-oon seemed more and more discomfited by the questions. By contrast, an odd sense of elation filled Gwi.

Perhaps something has gone wrong, he thought. Maybe the entire house deed was a flimsy excuse to come back down here. Gwi wondered what it might be. His imagination ran wild. Did he get in debt with the wrong people? Inappropriately involved with someone he shouldn't be?

"Come on," Gwi asked, leaning toward Ee-oon. Gwi's face felt hot, some mix of alcohol and excitement. "What's it like there? Surely it's better than here and my little dog farm."

Ee-oon laughed. "I've been meaning to talk to you about that—maybe I'll buy a dog before I leave."

"Oh," Gwi said. "I mean sure. I didn't know you liked dogs."

"No, no," Ee-oon said. "For the kid. I think she'll like it."

Gwi sat back down. "I didn't know that you had a kid."

"She'll be three this year."

Gwi took a long swig of his beer.

"So what is it that you do in Seoul?"

Ee-oon laughed. "I run a bookstore; can you believe that?"

Gwi tried to mime Ee-oon's laughter and failed. He asked a question instead. "Why did you steal them? Back then."

Ee-oon ruefully smiled and shrugged.

"It's just a dumb thing I did. It didn't mean anything."

"That's not true," Gwi murmured.

"I was just a kid making trouble."

"Bullshit," Gwi said.

The words came out angry, but he did not know why. Ee-oon did not push back. The sun began to set, and Gwi shuddered, remembering his dream earlier.

"Are you cold?" Ee-oon asked. Gwi seethed inside. It felt wrong, to sit here and be on the receiving end of Ee-oon's concern. Resentment and soju and pieces of pork belly were all mixing and sloshing about in Gwi's stomach.

"Why didn't you tell me?" Gwi asked after some time.

"I told you, it really didn't mean anything."

"Not the books," Gwi said. "About Seoul, about all the things you've been up to. You never once reached out."

Silence, short and sharp, like a canine, punctured the conversation.

"I'm not sure," Ee-oon said. "I guess I just wanted to focus on getting closure here."

Gwi's lips twisted.

"Must be nice."

He willed himself to not say the next words. They came slipping out of his mouth anyway. "To be able to wash your hands of it and leave."

Gwi expected anger, or for Ee-oon to at least be defensive. But the following words were kind, which was somehow worse.

"I mean, what stops you from doing the same?" Ee-oon asked.

"I've got my dogs," Gwi answered curtly.

Ee-oon made a sound somewhere between resignation and laughter.

"They aren't your dogs. You don't even like those dogs."

"Oh, piss off," Gwi said. "I love those dogs."

"Gwi, I've seen the dog farm. Heard you talk about it. You don't love those dogs."

"You don't know a fucking thing about me," Gwi snarled, then grew quiet, surprised at his own vehemence.

Ee-oon opened his mouth as if to say something, then nodded.

"So," Ee-oon said. "You love your dogs."

"Yes," Gwi snapped.

"Would this be the way you loved me when we were students?"

"What?" Gwi said. He felt the anger slipping out underneath him. Something awful was filling its void, something he could not place.

"Love? Who said anything about—"

"If you can't call it what it is, that's fine," Ee-oon said, waving a hand. "Is care better then? Is that how you cared? By telling my father that I planned to abandon him?"

"I didn't, I never said abandon—" Gwi stammered.

"For the longest time, I didn't get it," Ee-oon said. "Why you'd do something like that. I still didn't, not until I came here last week and saw your dogs."

Gwi tried to think of what to say. He thought of all the times he rehearsed this conversation in his mind. But they were of no use. Not once did he imagine that Ee-oon's voice would be this calm, this gentle.

"You say you care about your dogs," he said. "Based on what criteria? Because you use an incinerator instead of throwing their bodies into a ditch? Because you hose them down once a week instead of once a month?"

"I—"

He turned to Gwi and smiled wearily. He seemed to deflate, as if the years and events that had passed between them suddenly caught up to him in one moment.

"After all these years," he said. "Still hoarding broken things and mistaking pity for love."

The consequences of Gwi's words followed soon after.

One Tuesday, EMTs had swarmed his friend's house. A person

was wheeled out, but the EMTs roughly jostled Gwi out the way, making it impossible to see who it was. It was only later that Gwi found out what happened—attempted suicide via carbon monoxide.

Ee-oon did not come to school the next day, or the day after that. The teacher told the class that Ee-oon would be moving to Seoul, with that undertone that said do not ask questions.

The other kids swarmed Gwi's desk. They asked him things like *You were friends, do you know what happened?* and *Did Ee-oon tell you anything?*

But Gwi had no answers.

"I'm telling you, it was a murder-suicide attempt," one of the kids said.

"You don't know shit," a second kid said.

"Yes I do," retorted the first. "My father also works as an EMT."

"No way. Was he the one at the house?"

"No, but he was working that shift. He said it was yeontan poisoning."

"Hey, can you knock it off, I'm trying to take a nap," Gwi said.

The other boys ignored him and continued their discussion.

"Why do you think he did it?"

"Hey," Gwi shouted. "Can you go talk elsewhere and let me fucking sleep in peace?"

"You think it was because Ee-oon couldn't get into college?" a kid said.

"How do you know that it wasn't the other way around?"

another said. "What if Ee-oon was the one that lit the yeontan."

Gwi tackled the boy to the ground. By the time the teachers managed to separate them, Gwi's knuckles were raw and the other boy's face was a bloodied mess.

Gwi's hands were wet with perspiration. They kept slipping with the latch locks. One of the dogs, roused by his clumsy attempt, began to bark.

"Shut up," Gwi said. "Please shut up."

Other dogs took up the howling. An unbelievable cacophony rang up, so loud that Gwi was sure god himself would hear it.

"I'm trying to help, don't you get it," he said, first a whisper then a shout as the barking grew louder and louder. He clutched the wire cages with both hands and shook them so hard that his fingers bled. .

"Don't you fucking understand—please, please, I just want to help."

Gwi thought about letting them free, but that was not enough. He had to show Ee-oon. The dogs were fine. Hale and healthy. Gwi took good care of them; what the fuck did Ee-oon know? And what the fuck was all that about love that he had gone on about? Ee-oon was wrong, and it was easy to demonstrate it.

He went back to his car, but all he had were those blue plastic garbage bags. Gwi began shoving dogs into one. But filling the plastic bag with live dogs was an entirely different matter than filling it with dead ones. They fought, both against Gwi and each other. Claws tore holes into the bag. Muzzles erupted out of the torn holes. Speckles of blood began to spatter the inside of the bag. Still, Gwi continued to push more dogs into the bag.

"I'm just trying to get you out of here," he said. "It's because I care. I care. I promise I care."

He tied the bag and slung it over his back. The weight of it nearly drove him to his knees, but he got back up, bloodied fingers clutching the plastic garbage bag overflowing with dogs.

He drove with the bag sitting on the passenger seat. Filled to the brim like that with matted fur and teeth and howls, the plastic bag became something else entirely, a single creature that roared and writhed and bled.

"I just wanted to help," Gwi said, on the verge of tears. "I never meant any harm."

As Gwi got closer to his home, the sounds from the bag only grew louder. By the time he dragged the bag up two flights of stairs and stood in front of his house, the cacophony was awful and unearthly.

"Stop, stop, stop, stop," screamed Gwi.

The noise cut out, as if on cue. He dropped the bag and backed away. It lay there, utterly still. Gwi tried to peer into the bag, but it was too dark to see. He stood there as an indeterminable span of time passed. The plastic rustled in the grip of his violently shaking hands. With a cry, he tore it open.

There was nothing inside; the bag was entirely empty.

When Gwi opened his apartment door, it was dark—as dark as the inside of that plastic bag had been. Ee-oon was gone. He sank into the half-deflated air mattress. Soon, the sun would rise, long and jagged like teeth, and the dogs would begin to bark. He wondered how many such mornings lay stretched out before him.

AUTOPHAGY

P eased the scope further into the patient's stomach. The walls of flesh undulated slowly. He adjusted, following the gentle curve of the esophagus. His scalp itched. He wiped the sweat off his brow with his forearm, making sure his gloved hand did not touch skin. They were watching like hawks.

"Why bother removing it?" Cheongjin, from ENT, had said that morning. He sipped out of the Styrofoam cup, cheeks ballooning as he gargled the instant coffee. The liquid squeaked against his teeth.

"I mean, do we even know if it's malignant?"

He then idly began picking at a spot between his teeth with his hospital ID.

"What would you know," San said jokingly, raising a hand for a playful slap. "I don't see your degree from a university in Seoul."

San turned to P and smiled.

"Isn't that right?"

Thinly veiled hostility from Cheongjin was one thing, San's pretend amiability was another. San was a urologist and had the kind of smile that crinkled his eyes into slits. P did not trust those twin crescents. The hospital staff tiptoed around San. Partially because he was the only one who had gotten his degree from a med school within the capital. But mostly because he was the nephew of the hospital's chairman.

"Horse doctors," P muttered into his sanitary mask.

"Sorry, Doctor? I didn't catch that," said one of his assistants.

"Please tilt the head back a little further," P answered.

The throat widened into an amphitheater. P quickly found the polyp, looping the wire around the pale pink lump of flesh. He tightened the noose, feeling the snap on the tip of his fingers. It tore off with a small gout of blood and vanished into the patient's stomach.

"Wow, you got that in one go," said a resident.

P didn't mind the residents at Minjung General. It wasn't their fault they were working in this dump. Why kick a dog when it's down? But the compliments were too much. Their awe at every menial thing only further degraded him, a reminder of how low he had fallen. He used to appear on TV shows; now he was doing this.

He peeled his gloves off, hating the way perspiration caused the latex to stick to his fingers.

"Good work," he said to the pair, even though all they had done was stand around and gawk. He turned to leave.

"Um. Are we finished?" asked the shorter of the two, the one whose name started with J, or maybe G.

"This is a polyp removal surgery, yes?" asked P.

"Yes?"

"What did I just do?"

"Uh."

"Removed a polyp?" hazarded the taller one.

"Okay," P said, deliberately speaking very slowly as he took off his mask. "You tell me: Are we done?"

"Yes," the shorter one answered, turning pink.

"Okay, then."

It was a privilege to watch you work, the resident called out after him, twisting the knife further.

Back in his office, P pressed his forehead into the monitor, hands cradling the nape of his neck.

"Why the hell would you write a long-term prescription for Prilosec?" The words were nearly unintelligible through his clenched teeth. "No wonder she was growing polyps."

The previous physician had been a man named Hwee. P looked through the records to find Hwee had worked for Minjung General Hospital for nearly forty years before retiring two years ago. The hospital had seen fit to simply continue the patient's prescription. P felt resentful. He imagined calling up Hwee and taking out the day—no, the last three months—on him. The polyp had been completely benign, but he wanted to lie. *Hello, is this Hwee? Your patient's stomach polyps have blossomed into cancer. We cut out half her stomach and she's lost eight pounds in three weeks and she's dying as we speak, Hwee, you worthless piece of shit.*

He turned the computer off and looked at his phone. There were two texts from Seona, his wife.

can you pick up some beef on your way home, read the first.

it's okay if you can't, read the other.

"Seventeen months," he said to himself. P could feel his spirits rising. It wasn't that much time after all. "Only seventeen."

On the way home, he dropped by the butcher shop and got some beef. He even managed to whistle a little.

P could not have possibly imagined how all-consuming a thing like humidity could be. It wasn't something solved by swapping undershirts in the middle of the shift or leaving the fan on overnight.

Three weeks after moving in, runny stains appeared on the

upper rim of the bathroom sink, in that little crevice where the marble of the cabinet met the porcelain. The toilet soon followed suit.

P offered to do the cleaning, insisted on it. He bought Clorox and doused the bathroom until his head swam with that slippery smell, but the ochre stains only grew larger, slowly darkening into burnt grease.

When he called the maintenance to complain, the man who showed up took one look and told P it was just mold.

"All this water in the air."

"Well, do something about it," P snapped.

The man paused and searched P's face. His eyes were small and wet.

"You diabetic?"

P stood at a loss for words.

"Diabetics piss sugar. Black mold loves it."

Everything about the exchange put him off, from the man's crass comments to the casual way he ran his bare fingers across the mold. He attempted to clean it again a couple more times. P retched as he scrubbed the toilet. But the mold never failed to grow back, water and porcelain transubstantiating into that slippery living rust. He soon gave up. Now when P leaned into the sink to wash his face each morning, the side of his hand would sometimes brush the moldy porcelain. He'd shudder or curse. The mold was the true tenant of his house.

The city held other surprises. P found himself waking earlier each day. Even if he could ignore the damp of the house, he could not do the same with the cicadas. Day after day, P saw more holes on the ground, tunnels left behind by the emerging insects. He stomped on them in frustration, but their bodies smeared and crumbled beneath his feet in a way that haunted him.

"It's only February," P whispered.

But the cicadas of H City did not care, and neither did anyone else. Cars simply drove over the swarms. Dirt from unpaved roads mixed with bent wings and yellowish insect blood. The crushed remains did not desiccate under the watery sun of H City, but instead grew putrid until the wild dogs got to them.

P recalled how nervous his previous hospital's director looked when he broke the news.

"It'll be just for a little," he said, wringing his hands then wiping them on his pants. P stared at the dark hand-shaped stain of perspiration. "H City is a good place to relax."

"I don't understand," P had said. "Why am I getting relocated when Jeong-min is the problem?"

The director made a face, equal parts supplication and grimace.

"I'm sorry, P. Consider it an extended vacation," the director had said. "Duck it out for a little while, until all of this blows over. By summer next year, you'll be back, and no one will be the wiser."

A year and a half in H City. The realtor had called the city rural but charming, quiet without being too provincial.

P had imagined something different. He had grown up in the countryside, after all. His grandparents had raised a cow. P imagined open horizons that sloped gently. Fields of wheat. Maybe the occasional smell of manure. Peaceful, even dreary—but with its own kind of beauty.

On their last day in J City, he lay in bed and told his wife what he imagined it to be like.

Like a Wyeth painting, she said, but her back was turned to him. He did not know who Wyeth was. She did not explain further.

Many patients in H City came to see P, mostly for endoscopy or colonoscopy.

"You're very popular," the nurse had joked.

It wasn't anything to brag about. There simply hadn't been anyone to give such examinations in H City. The population had been slowly stagnating during the past two years; no one was applying to be a GI doctor at Minjung General Hospital. But there was still a kind of satisfaction. From time to time, the feeling of being needed almost distracted P from the injustice of what happened.

Lunch at the cafeteria consisted of beef and quail eggs braised with soy sauce. The side dish was lotus roots. San set his tray next to him.

"I'm very grateful that you chose to come to our hospital of all places," he said. "Dr. Hwee's departure left us pretty understaffed."

The lotus root crunched against San's teeth. P did not like how they looked, those neat clusters of holes.

Hospitals in places like H City were territorial. Insular. It was an atmosphere that bred distrust of outsiders. And corruption. Odds were someone was overbilling in medical supply insurance claims, or asking patients for informal payments that went unlogged. Under-the-table propofol shots always made good money, but they probably did not have the guts to go that far.

"So, what made you pick our city?" San asked.

Both he and P understood that one did not work in a large hospital in the capital and then suddenly relocate to a place like H City. Not willingly, anyhow. P knew what San was up to. He was probing P for weakness, or maybe leverage. Something to keep P's mouth shut, should he find out about whatever shady things they were up to.

You're wasting your time, P thought. He was not here to stay. This was a minor inconvenience, something he and his wife would look back and laugh about. A year and a half and they could return to J City, to their previous lives.

"Just needed a change of scenery," P answered, the overcooked rice pasting into mush in his mouth.

When P came home, Seona was preparing dinner, a bag of instant curry powder next to the stove.

"Instant," he remarked, the words not precisely an accusation. Seona had always given him shit for eating instant.

"I wanted curry," she answered. Beside her was a bowl filled with some kind of ground meat. P did not know what animal it was from; he was not a good cook. "But they didn't have any turmeric or cumin in the store," she said, mincing the garlic into a paste. "What kind of a supermarket doesn't carry spice?"

P took his shirt off, struggling as the wet fabric clung to his back. He avoided his wife's eyes. It was not his fault that they had to relocate, but that applied doubly to Seona. She did not have to be here.

"Don't use the shower," Seona said without raising her head from the cutting board.

"What?"

"Something's wrong with the water boiler. It stinks."

"I've been outside all day."

"Use cold water then. The warm water reeks of sulfur."

P grew irritated. He thought about arguing, and then looked at Seona, at the hair that stuck to her face. He walked up to her, using a thumb to wipe the perspiration off her cheeks.

"What?" asked Seona. She looked up and tried to shrug his hand away.

"Okay, okay," P answered, tucking in the stray hair strands behind her ear. He remembered that none of this was her fault. It wasn't his either, but that did not warrant giving her a hard time. She smiled despite herself, and P smiled too.

They talked over dinner. How his day had been ("One abdominal abscess, two endoscopies, and a rash of stomach flu"). How her dissertation was going ("Not easy but manageable"). P complained about Cheongjin and his disgusting coffee-gargling habit ("Ugh, I bet his teeth are all stained too"), Seona's obstinate thesis committee ("Really, what difference does a remote dissertation defense make?"). It was its own kind of intimacy, being irritated at the same shitty people together.

"Hey, let's open the wine," he said suddenly. "The good stuff that we got over Christmas last year."

"What, now?" Seona said. "What's the occasion?"

"No occasion."

They polished off that bottle then opened another. The wine dried their mouths and stained their teeth. They laughed and danced until their foreheads were beaded with sweat. And for a moment, P was convinced that everything was going to be alright.

Seona began nodding off and eventually retreated to the bedroom, yawning.

"Not sleeping yet?" she asked.

"I'll just finish this," he said, waving the half empty bottle.

"Okay," she answered. "Don't stay up too late."

P made a noncommittal noise. He thought of work, then slowly deflated, his good mood leaving him. He did not want to go to bed, to end the day and start the cycle all over again.

Seventeen months, he thought again to himself. But the span of time felt much longer than it did a couple days ago.

The wine beside him now sat untouched. He scrolled through video after video on his computer. He watched an elephant picking up a stick to imitate a rhino. A video about the life cycle of the sunfish. A news article about a livestock virus. A livestream where a man sat in a sparely furnished, dimly lit room—not much different from the one P was in now—and ate sickening amounts of raw fish. The alcohol from earlier gurgled in his stomach uncomfortably as he stared at the man's teeth, slippery and red with gochujang.

H City exported pigs. They outnumbered the city's population a hundred to one. P didn't know where the farms and abattoirs were, exactly, but he could tell they were there. They'd smelled it on their drive down. Something too physical to be considered an odor—there was metaphysical mass to the scent. It coated the back of their tongues with a chemical stickiness. Twice, Seona had to stop and retch.

The swine were ubiquitous. The city paraded pig mascots. Stores sold pig souvenirs. Restaurants painted them onto their signs. Rosy pigs in chef's hats and sly grins, pigs nudging each other and winking. Pigs in checkered aprons with one hand rubbing their bellies and the other raised, holding a silver cloche. What was beneath the dome of stainless steel? What warranted the knowing wink? P did not want to know.

Sometimes farmers visited the hospital for a checkup and left their trucks in the parking lot, still loaded with livestock. The pigs in those trucks were not the soft, indolent things that the city advertised itself with. They were prodigious. Heat radiated off their bodies, with hides as dark as the fat flies that swarmed around their tear ducts. They were not afraid of P, roaring and snapping at his hand when he approached. He did not like how square and human their molars were. *They have eyelashes,* he realized, and somehow this of all things was the tipping point at which the smell got to him. He reeled away, gagging.

But still, it seemed doable. A year and a half was, in the grand scheme of things, a flash in the pan.

"I mean, think of how long you were in med school to get here," Seona told him while he packed their lunch. "All those asses you kissed. This should be nothing compared to that."

P flicked a grape at her, and she laughed.

They went out for drives during the weekend. There was a coastline about an hour away from the city.

"Hey," P suddenly said as they sat by the water. "I'm sorry about all this. That it all went down the way it did."

She nodded. Her expression was something odd, a face that P had never seen before.

"Hey P," she said after a while. "If you had known that this would happen, would you have still done it?"

"What do you mean?"

"Would you still blow the whistle."

"I mean, he was stealing money from the hospital—*our* hospital."

Her jaw quietly moved, as if she was chewing over her words. Eventually, she flashed P a wan smile and nodded briskly.

"I see," was all she said.

She spent the ride back with her forehead pressed to the car's window. P glanced at her from time to time but could not tell if she was asleep or not.

It did not take long for P to realize that the pigs were not the true problem. It was what came of the pigs.

Byproduct from a million and a half pigs were collected and dumped into massive open-air septic tanks. Guts, feces, urine, and blood all flowed into massive lagoons, too viscous to be fully liquid. When the wind blew, the surface quivered. Some things floated to the top; most sank. The tanks often overflowed during monsoon season.

Mosquitoes and horse flies swarmed to lay their eggs in the fetid water. Bullfrogs devoured the white clumps of eggs, and in turn, were eaten by herons. Twitching bodies spindled upon bright yellow beaks, all of it speckled with blood.

People swapped rumors. About pigs that escaped the cages, and how they grew feral. Large enough to kill wild dogs and hungry enough to devour anything. Several years before, a landslide collapsed a section of the city's cemetery. Not all the bodies could be accounted for. People blamed the wild pigs, whispered that the bodies of their friends and family had vanished into the cavernous dark of a pig's stomach. A year after that, a child went missing. The police concluded that she had been playing near the waste reservoir and slipped. Her father was convinced the pigs tore her apart. It was all the same. One way or another, H City had devoured her.

When the reservoirs grew full, they were siphoned and run through giant, howling machines that rendered everything to liquid. It became fertilizer for the corn that they fed the pigs. Pigs that ate pigs that ate pigs that ate pigs. The liquified remains were expelled onto the corn farms with massive sprinklers. It rained pigs in H City.

The rule was that P made breakfast and his wife made dinner, and that they ate with minimal complaint. It wasn't a rule that needed reinforcing; neither was a picky eater and both knew what the other liked.

He made eggs that morning. An omelet for him and two sunny-side ups for her. Two slices of toast each. Ketchup for P, soy sauce for her. The same way she had taken eggs for the last eight years.

He set the plates on the dining table, which was nearly covered end to end with her books and manuscripts. He began eating by himself. She did not look up from her monitor until he was nearly finished. She took a couple of half-hearted bites before pushing the food to the side.

"What's wrong?"

"I'm just not really feeling eggs today," Seona answered.

His wife looked tired. She had lost nearly eight pounds in two months. There was no cancer or tumor to account for the loss. It was just H City. Her collarbone jutted out in a way that made P think of fingers pressed against fabric. Her skin was thin and taut, cling wrap stretched around packaged meat.

"Let me know if you want anything else," P said while washing the dishes. P stared at the strands of still-runny yolk from Seona's plate mixing with the water and sighed.

The next day, a patient came in for stomach surgery.

P cut into the peritoneum. There was a soft hiss as air escaped the cavity. The assistant gagged. Congealed chunks of partially digested blood glistened black under the surgical light.

"I told you that you weren't applying enough Tiger Balm on your mask," P said without looking over.

There were no harmonic scalpels in Minjung General, only those older electrosurgery units. P had forgotten how much surgical smoke the body emitted with electrosurgery. Skin, adipose, and muscle burned away into a spray of fine mist. A person sublimating on the spot—a vanishing trick if there ever was one.

P thought of the pigs. The way they rooted around in the mud and breathed air with a million dead pigs in it. For the first time in over ten years, the smell of the surgery broke him. It filled his lungs, leaving no room for air. He could taste the man's gangrene at the back of his throat. He gagged and staggered out of the surgery room.

Later in the break room, San came up to him, hand outstretched to offer a cup of coffee. His eyes were creased in a smile. He had seen what happened. P knew what lay behind the gesture, the smug satisfaction at P's fuckup. He had just bolted out of surgery like a rookie.

"It happens," San said.

P ignored the cup and walked out, seething.

P sat in his living room with a glass of iced water pressed to his forehead. Seona stood by the kitchen counter, mincing leeks for jeon.

"Are you at least going to tell me what happened?"

He thought about telling her, about what the man's rotting guts had smelled like, about pigs that ate pigs—but his stomach churned again, and he took a shaky sip of his water instead.

"I left early," he answered, the words clipped. "Felt unwell."

"I thought you had surgery today," she said.

"I'm going to take a shower," P said, walking toward the bathroom.

"Don't use the hot water."

"You'll live."

The knife slammed into the table. Bits of leek went careening off the cutting board. A fleck landed on her cheek. She seemed to not notice. The silence between them sagged like an overripe fig.

"Please."

The old guilt almost stirred, but somewhere down the line, it had ossified into something hard. Brittle.

"Fine."

By the time he came out, his teeth were chattering. Seona pushed a plate of leek jeon, some gesture of conciliation. But he wordlessly shook his head; he had no appetite.

In the end, it wasn't the heat or the humidity that broke the people of H City. It wasn't half a million cicadas emerging two months early or the squealing of pigs or the thundering of machines. It wasn't even the smell. The reason ended up being disappointingly anticlimactic.

"There's just no more money to be made," the patient told P.

His breath was hot and smelled faintly of garlic and alcohol. He told P about the livestock virus that was sweeping the countryside. That the government was mandating all affected livestock to be killed in an effort to prevent any further spread.

"Do you want to know what we do with the pigs once we kill them?"

P did not say yes. The man shared anyway.

"We burn them."

P and Seona sat in the kitchen. Both were yelling. Skin had formed on their soup.

"I *told* you. It's just until next year, and then—"

"I know." Her mouth twisted. "Just until next year and then

they'll relocate you back to J City, and you can once again be a hotshot GI doctor that gets invited to be a TV show panelist. All the while my committee thinks I'm fucking insane for doing a long-distance dissertation and my thesis is ruined."

"How could you blame me for this?" P asked.

"Who else could I blame?"

"It wasn't me who embezzled from the hospital."

Frustration deepened the lines around Seona's mouth. She opened and closed her mouth several times, then with resignation, spoke.

"Face it, P, you didn't speak up out of any sense of justice."

It wasn't true. Yes, his colleague had been a sore spot for years, always undermining P's position. Always embarrassing him in public and speaking ill behind his back. But that wasn't why P had reported him. The man was a parasite and the world deserved to know it.

"You just disliked him. That was all. You wanted to see him humiliated."

"How could I know he'd turn it around on me? That he would get me relocated?"

Seona laughed. P did not like the strange glow of her eyes. Too bright. Avian, somehow. His wife reminded P of the herons that stalked the ragged clumps of bulrush.

"Don't be naive, P."

"What are you talking about."

"You tell the hospital director about an insurance fraud your colleague was committing. He tells you he will sort it out."

He no longer found his wife desirable. She frightened him, with her disheveled hair and anemic veins straining against her neck. But more than her appearance, it was how she sat across him now, fists curled. Every fiber of her being was a silent accusation—and it was that accusation, more than anything, that scared him.

"Two weeks later, he tells you they want to avoid a large investigation and asks you to relocate to this shithole for a year and a half. The guy you blew the whistle on walks scot-free."

"Stop," P said. "I don't want to hear it."

"Think, P. They fucked you. They were all in it together."

P wanted to sweep everything off the table. He wanted to shake Seona and scream at her face.

"Now you're angry," she said, laughing again. "You're a lot angrier now than you were when I told you about my thesis committee. How they said moving could jeopardize my entire defense."

She stood up, took the soup, and poured it down the drain.

"I think you care more that they got the better of you," she said. "A lot more than what you did to us."

"I didn't do this," P shouted. "They did this. They did it to me."

She shut the door to the bedroom. P walked into the bathroom and blasted hot water over his itching head until his eyes watered with the stench of rotting eggs.

The next day during work, P's phone buzzed.

i'm staying with my parents.

P was in the middle of eating lunch by himself in a convenience store when he got the phone call.

"Who is this?" he asked with a mouthful of sandwich.

"This is the police department of H City, District 3."

"Oh," he answered, puzzled.

"We're calling about your wife."

The tuna in the sandwich tasted old, the texture a gritty paste against the roof of his mouth. His lips were dry.

"Oh."

"We received a call from her parents. They claim that your wife left H City to stay with them."

"Yeah, she left," he said, catching himself before he could finish the sentence and say *me*. "What do you mean *they claim*?"

"Well, they're claiming that she never arrived at J City, sir."

So, even she had turned on him. Or maybe it was her parents—they had never really liked him. P could easily imagine them phoning the police, feigning concern. It would look better in the divorce courts, make it seem like she fled from P in a panic.

"So what are you implying," he snapped. "That I lopped her head off and stuck it in formaldehyde?"

There was a shocked silence.

"Sir, we're just calling to let you know what happened."

P hung up and walked back to the hospital.

The government began setting up emergency checkpoints. The sunlight, filtered through the clouds of aerosol bactericide, seemed ashen. Haggard men in hazmat suits swarmed cars at sanitation zones like ants on a sugar cube, hoses of disinfectant at hand.

H City smelled of chemical disinfection. But beneath lingered that old smell, that of dead pigs. More pigs were dying than ever. *Swift euthanasia of all affected livestock is crucial for containment*, read government pamphlets. Farmers on the verge of tears ushered hundreds of pigs into makeshift plastic gas chambers and pumped them full of CO_2. But it was a drop in the bucket, nowhere near enough. More pigs had to go. More, more, more, and more.

They quickly gave up on incineration; there were too many for that. Burying was proposed as an alternative. Diggers converted open fields into mass graves. Trucks unloaded hundreds of dead pigs into the holes, already stinking. In a different city, a quarantine worker suddenly collapsed and died. Some said that it was from overwork. Others said that he had a heart attack after falling into a pit of bloated bodies.

P had come home one day to see a cloud of fruit flies swarming the half-finished glass of wine on his desk. When he emptied the glass, dead flies clung to the side.

His war with the tiny insects began. No matter how many

traps he bought, how many sprays he used, more arrived. He would wash and set the dishes to dry, only to wash them again after seeing the tiny spots of black scuttling over the plates.

Sometimes he'd slap his hands to kill them. Watching the bugs idly fly away was infuriating. Opening his hands to see a smear still twitching on his palm was hardly better.

The mold continued spreading. A halo of grayish blue began blooming around the lid of the washing machine. The drying rack in the kitchen suffered the same fate. Everything was slippery to the touch, raw fat against his fingers.

The police continued to harass P. They had called his landlord, who told them that P and his wife had fought often. P was not surprised that the landlord had been eavesdropping.

"Nosy prick," he said to himself.

The police asked about what happened in J City, and P had nearly screamed at the injustice of it. They thought he'd fled J City after some sort of scandal.

"Eleven months," P dully told himself as he ate his dinner. The chicken was burnt, but he did not have the energy to cook another.

There was something wrong with P's patient. The man never stopped talking, all of it in a constant whisper. His left eye was suffering from a cataract, the center of his pupil misshapen. P's hand remained suspended between them, unshaken. The man wore a pair of black pinstripe pants two sizes too big for his wizened frame.

They were pulled up to his ribs. He was balding, and whoever had dyed what was left of his white hair black had done a shoddy job.

"I told you, it's no use," said the man who stood next to him. "He's not all there."

"Sorry, who are you?" he asked.

"I'm his son-in-law," he said. The old man began reaching for P's stethoscope and the other man slapped down his hand.

"Don't do that," he snapped, then apologized. "He gets like this when he's in here."

The old man made another move, this time for P's computer. The man slapped his hand again with an audible crack.

"Please stop hitting him," P said reflexively. "Can you please give me some privacy with the patient?"

"Suit yourself," the younger man said, ambling out.

The man proved very difficult to talk to. P gathered that his stomach and throat were hurting but could understand little beyond that. He seemed to want to talk about everything, all in that register of garbled whisper.

"When I was a kid," the old man said, mumbling on despite the tongue compressor in his mouth. "Way way back when I was a little kid they assigned me homework to catch grasshopper . . . it was for a show-and-tell and I caught them . . . they were a pest for the crops and I caught twenty-six."

He only stopped talking for brief, ragged gasps of air.

"I caught twenty-six and I was very proud . . . they were going to give a prize to whoever caught the most and that was me . . . I put them all in a little empty cookie box over the weekend."

His cloudy left eye was transfixed on P's face. P felt dizzy. *Ten months and two weeks,* he thought. The room felt very small.

"Sir," P spoke, interrupting the man. "I'm sorry but I didn't catch your name."

The babbling ceased. The man handed over a scrunched piece of paper.

It read: *Hello my name is Hwee. If I appear disoriented or lost, please*—The rest of the card was stained and illegible. Hwee continued to babble.

P simply decided on a diagnosis. Acid reflux. He felt a twinge of guilt, but he did not want to look at his predecessor anymore, did not want to peer into the man's insides to find out what forty years of H City did to a doctor.

"I just taped the box shut and left it in my room over the weekend . . . during the entire weekend and a weird sound kept coming out of the box."

P scribbled out a prescription but his hands, clammy with perspiration, kept spelling things wrong.

"I couldn't sleep because something from inside the box kept scratching and nobody believed me . . . not my mother or father they just said shut up."

P's head itched. The dermatologist had said it was heat rash and told him to dry his hair completely before going to bed. But his wife had taken the hair dryer with her when she left, and nothing dried in this city anyway, everything was wet and sticky and Hwee would not stop talking.

"One night I couldn't take it and I finally opened the box . . . there weren't twenty-six grasshoppers . . . would you like to know what was inside?"

P did not want to know. He just wanted to be elsewhere. Ten months and two weeks. Ten months was forty-three weeks; he could just do away with the two weeks. What was fourteen days anyway?

"There was just one grasshopper . . . one massive grasshopper with only four legs left . . . it jumped into my face and vanished behind the closet and from then on I could never really sleep properly . . . I kept hearing the scratching the scratching from that one final grasshopper that had gobbled up all the other grasshoppers . . . I could hear it in the dark."

Hwee looked on the verge of tears.

"I think that this is sad, isn't it really really sad—that one grasshopper that had to eat and eat and eat but what else could it do? It was either eat or be eaten and so it ate and ate and ate until there was nothing left."

They didn't even bother killing the pigs anymore. Farmers, now destitute, were in no mood to adhere to sanitation protocols. It was illegal, but they did it anyway. Dump trucks drove up to the mass graves at night and spilled live pigs into the dirt.

Grouped together by the hundreds, the struggling bodies no longer looked like individual things. Each pit became a singular, massive, writhing beast, animated by an ocean of death and dying. The ground bubbled and frothed from the fluid escaping the carcasses. Wild dogs that attempted to dig up the mound had their skulls caved in with shovels. They, too, were fed to the pits.

Dirt was hastily thrown on top, but it was not enough. This was too much, even for H City. As the bodies decomposed, the earth began swelling from the corpse gas, as if to protest. Impregnated by corpses, the ground distended. Instead of cicadas, other things started to emerge. Snouts, hooves, and spines bloomed.

P was very drunk when he got the call. Although it was an unsaved number, he could tell by the area code that it was the police. No one else called him now.

"What?" he demanded, words slurred. "What the fuck do you want?"

"Sir," the voice said, and even through his drunken haze, P could hear the hesitance behind it. "Did your spouse have a small birthmark near her left ankle?"

P could not remember.

"What is this about?"

The man told P a body had been found.

"It's not Seona," P said instantly.

"Sir, I understand that this might be difficult, but we need to know if your wife had a birthmark near her left ankle."

"I—I don't know." It was hard to think. A fruit fly buzzed near his hand. He slapped at it, missing and shattering the cup on his desk. "Seona had an appendectomy. There should be a scar near her lower stomach."

There was a very long pause over the phone.

"We only found a leg. It seems," the man paused, barely managing to avoid saying *your wife*. "Someone had fallen into the pig waste cesspool. They only fished out the one leg."

P threw the phone against the wall. He vaguely heard it shatter. It wasn't Seona. There was no way it could be. They weren't the same as the dead-eyed inhabitants of H City. Those people that walked by the abattoirs unfazed, inured to the smell of pigs and death—those people that ate pigs and then were eaten by pigs in turn.

"That's not me," he said. "That's not us."

They would get out.

He tried to sit back down but could not keep still.

"Okay," he said. "Okay. What's the harm in going to check? It's not her, so it's fine. It'll be fine."

He was too drunk to drive, but the address the officer had given him was within walking distance. He staggered out of the house and began to walk. The moonlight was hazy, although he could not tell if it was clouds or chemical aerosol. Soon, P began running. The faster he got to the morgue, the faster he could put it behind him, he reasoned. It wasn't Seona anyway. His wife was fine. He was fine. It was all going to work out. He realized at some point that he had stumbled off the sidewalk and onto the road, but he continued to run. It had rained earlier, and the night air was heavy. But underneath was that ubiquitous smell—that of pigs. It grew stronger until P had to stop, doubling over to half gasp for air and half gag.

From behind, a horn blared. The car clipped him on the shoulder and P felt the inevitable tipping as he lost his balance and fell into one of the enormous holes dug for the pigs.

He felt his leg shatter upon the impact. He screamed and tried to crawl his way out, but the precarious ground, soft with the fluid from the rotting pigs, shifted under his weight. He continued to sink.

P tried distracting himself from the pain by calculating how much time he had left in H City. Forty-three weeks. How many days were in forty-three weeks?

He heard a car stop beside the pit.

"Help," P screamed. "There's someone down here."

Seven days in a week. Twenty-four hours in a day. Seven times forty-three times twenty-four.

He heard the truck beep as its hydraulics strained. And then it was raining pigs. He screamed again but the sound was thin and reedy against the incredible din. Screaming bodies tumbled and whirled into the chasm. Something sticky dribbled down the nape of his neck. He vomited but could not smell it. All that filled his lungs were pigs, dead and dying; they blotted out the sky. P looked all around him, but he could no longer tell where he ended and the pigs began.

STRUCTURAL

FAILURES

There was a stain on Sak-hee's jacket, a dull shade of brown. He-jin stared at the stain and thought of Sak-hee sitting cramped in front of a desk for long hours. Months, years, decades of overtime, until his urine turned a mahogany brown.

It was probably soy sauce, but urine felt more appropriate. Sak-hee was one of those desert animals, one of those turtles that pissed once a month and had eyes like cracked kaleidoscopes.

Her cousins had raised one. He-jin remembered her shock at how quickly its jaws could snap.

"Sak-hee, you've got a little bit of, uh—" she said. She tried to gesture with her elbow, balancing the stack of documents with her arms at the same time. Several sheets fell.

"Damn it, He-jin," Sak-hee said, picking up the papers. "What is it?"

"You've got a stain there."

"Oh."

Sak-hee looked down and rubbed at the stain, sending dried bits flaking off. He-jin stared at the uneven circle of dwindling hair. The old urge came back, the one that gripped her ever since Sak-hee's overly warm hand first wrapped itself around He-jin's. She wanted to slap the top of her boss's head. She wouldn't hit him very hard; the want did not stem from a desire to hurt the man.

It would be such a satisfying sound, He-jin thought.

But satisfaction was a distant and foreign concept in the City Hall Department of Architecture. The only sound here was that of shuffling paper or the occasional hum of the Xerox machine. There was a constant odor that just bordered on being unpleasant—years of instant coffee and dust.

Aside from that, the rest consisted of work. There was always another illegal food stall to fine or a permit that needed issuing. They tore things down and built taller and better things in their stead, bloating the skyline inch by concrete inch. Architecture in

Municipality K proliferated the way duckweed and pond scum bloomed in stagnant lakes.

He-jin idly imagined slamming her palm down, right on top of the Sak-hee's bald pate, which was currently reflecting the sickly LED ceiling lights. The sound of flesh against flesh cutting through the white noise—then silence. The quiet in that aftermath would be of a different kind, something irrevocably changed by her action.

Instead, He-jin politely looked away while Sak-hee applied saliva to the stain.

"Thanks," he said. "Hey, you got any of the land registry forms? I think mine ran out."

"I think Senior Assistant Paeng has them," He-jin replied as she walked toward the break room. "I'll ask."

Sak-hee called after her, "If you're grabbing coffee, can you get me a cup? Extra cream and sugar."

He-jin did not drink coffee. It had been eight months and four days since she last had any. She'd quit after she passed her civil service exams. She'd had enough coffee to last a lifetime during the four years she spent studying. Everyone in the office knew it, but Sak-hee either did not remember or simply did not care.

In the break room, He-jin watched the anemic strains of the creamer blurring with the black. Her fingers tightened. It took conscious effort to not crush the Styrofoam cup.

It was nearly nine o'clock by the time He-jin gathered her things to leave. She checked to see if Jin-ee had texted her, but her phone was empty.

There had been a rainstorm earlier. Gray water and the last dregs of August were circling the sewage gutters, but the heat was reluctant to leave the city. By the time He-jin arrived at Hanmaeum goshiwon, her jacket hung limply from her shoulder, her shirt damp with sweat.

She stood outside the goshiwon, her home. Many such buildings littered Municipality K.

"This one is an original, though," Soo had told He-jin. "Lots of students studied here and went off to become big. It's a good location. If you know geomancy, you'd know."

It was a relic from a bygone age. Built in the nineties when the city was just starting to turn into a hub for exam preppers, her goshiwon was a drab three-story affair that thirty or so people called home. The third floor was for women only, while the first two were for the men.

Many of the tenants were high school graduates who did not get into a good college, often referred to as restudies. Others studied for the bar or, like He-jin, for the civil service entrance exams.

But over time, a goshiwon had the same effect on a person. Exhausted, harried-looking faces milled about the common rooms. They took the bus to Dongdaemun and bought cheap wholesale clothing. When the neck holes stretched and loosened, they scrunched up the fabric with rubber bands.

He-jin walked toward the entrance but stopped when a flash of light blinded her. Soo, who doubled as the building administrator and the guard, stood inside, shining his flashlight into her face.

"Who's that?" he asked.

It was purely out of spite. He knew who she was. She had been at Hanmaeum almost as long as he had been. But he still blinded her whenever he had the chance.

"You're still here?" he asked.

He made a face, creasing the bridge of his nose. He-jin thought of bell peppers, the way they grew wrinkly and soft when left too long in the fridge. He gave her a suspicious once-over.

"You don't look like you were out studying."

"It was work," she answered curtly.

"Work? Like moonlighting at a café?" he asked. "You have your priorities wrong."

He opened the door to let her in, shaking his head.

"You should be studying. How are you going to pass your exams at this rate?" he said.

It took some effort, but He-jin managed to keep her breathing even. She reached into her pocket and thumbed her city hall ID, which comforted her. What did he know, after all? He was just a dead-end goshiwon administrator, venting his spleen out on someone else. She had already passed the exams, months ago. There was a fierce stab of satisfaction at this thought, tinged with shame—the latter of which she quickly dismissed. It was neither illegal nor immoral to stay at a goshiwon after passing your exams. No one did so, but that didn't make her wrong.

She turned and smiled.

"Goodnight!"

The man sucked in air through his teeth, as if disappointed that she could not be goaded into an argument. He clicked the flashlight off, leaving He-jin to stand in the dark until the twin doors of the elevator opened and filled her face with fluorescence, that shade of yellow that she associated with legal pads. She leaned her head against the elevator, feeling it rattle as it took her up to her home.

"If my life amounted to cleaning kimchi stains off a goshiwon communal kitchen, I'd be an asshole too," she muttered.

On her first day of work at the Department of Architecture, Sak-hee had bought He-jin lunch.

"It's protocol around here," he said. "Supervisor buys the rookie lunch on their first day."

He did not ask what she wanted to eat.

"There's a good galbitang place," he said.

Sak-hee ordered his with extra broth and twice the meat. He-jin meekly ordered the regular. In no time, two stone pots filled with boiling hot soup were served. Sak-hee's was so large that it could have been used as a washbasin. He ate ravenously, his teeth deftly tearing chunks of meat off the bones. He only paused to take a long, noisy swig of water and to dab at his ever-reddening face with the flimsy paper napkins on the table.

"No need for ceremonies," he said. "Dig in."

She ate enough to be polite, then pushed the food around with her spoon. Mostly, she stared at the pile of used napkins as they slowly uncrumpled. Flecks of green onion and grains of rice were stuck to their edges.

"You know," Sak-hee said, his spoon scraping the bottom of the bowl. "You aren't what I expected. What university did you graduate from? One of the big three? Or Seo-kuk?"

He-jin told her supervisor that she was from neither, that she wasn't even from a university within the capital. She felt her face coloring from embarrassment. But Sak-hee did not seem to notice.

"Nothing wrong with a good school, of course," he said. "But sometimes, kids come out with their heads filled with useless things. In some ways, a shit school is good."

He-jin sat still, shocked at Sak-hee's crassness. He shrugged.

"It's true," he said. "It keeps you grounded. What buildings do you like?"

"Sorry?"

"Well, you applied for the department of construction and architecture. You don't have any interest in architecture?"

He-jin began to stammer something about Gaudí, tripping over her words, but Sak-hee interrupted her.

"Trick question," he said. "I mean it's good to care, I guess, but that's not what you'll do here. You're here to approve buildings, not be some hotshot rockstar architect."

There was an undercurrent of condescension in his voice that irked He-jin. She wasn't an idiot; she knew what she had applied for. She held no illusions about being a Gaudí—at least not here.

"Where are you from?" he asked.

"I actually spent the last four years here," she answered. "A goshiwon. I was preparing for the civil service exam."

Sak-hee grimaced. "Goddamn eyesores," he said. "They're the reason why land prices won't go up around here."

He wasn't wrong, but goshiwons and Municipality K were inseparable. They had formed an ecosystem of their own. Students flocked to the cheap housing. Like wood ears growing on a rotting stump, business followed suit—it wasn't anything glamorous, but it was money. Coin laundries with study desks. Unmanned self-convenience stores. Streets outside the large central subway station of Municipality K were always riddled with food carts, all of them varying degrees of illegal. They packed greasy Styrofoam bowls full of Spam and fried kimchi. Affordable, fast, and expendable were the cardinal virtues of Municipality K.

They talked a bit more, or more accurately, Sak-hee talked at He-jin while she only half listened. She stared at Sak-hee's mouth. One of his incisors was an implant. The ceramic was yellow, stained by some combination of time, cigarettes, and coffee.

He-jin had put her chopsticks down, but Sak-hee made no motion to leave. He ordered beer, and leisurely began to sip. Before

He-jin could say something, a mousy man with slicked hair sat next to her.

The man had watery eyes, wore a suit, and had nails that were trimmed very short—to the point that a patch of the tender flesh was visible. The man quickly assessed He-jin.

"Who's this?"

"Just helping the new hire adjust."

The man turned to Sak-hee and spoke while the other man drank his beer in silence. There was something smug about the way Sak-hee let the other man nervously ramble. He-jin's stomach gurgled with hunger. She lamented not eating more lunch.

They talked a while more. The conversation remained trivial.

"So, there should be no problem, then?" he asked Sak-hee.

"Everything looks fine and accounted for," Sak-hee answered. "The permit should be out within the week. It's all just protocol."

When the other man left, He-jin noticed the car and the chauffeur waiting for him outside the building. The car gleamed deadly and chrome against the sun. It looked very expensive.

"Who was that?" she asked Sak-hee.

"A secretary for one of the senior directors at WG Construction," Sak-hee said. He said it with a degree of expectation, as if He-jin should be impressed.

"That's—that's one of the biggest construction companies in the country."

Despite everything, Sak-hee was right; a small part of He-jin was impressed.

"Yes," he answered, his voice distant and distracted now.

He walked over to the other side of the table and sat in the now empty seat. When he lifted the cup of coffee, He-jin saw that the other man had left behind an envelope. It was very full. When Sak-hee noticed He-jin staring, he shrugged.

"Work hard enough and one day you'll be having meetings of your own," he said, then smiled.

His false teeth dully caught the light. For a moment, He-jin debated walking out. Yes, it was true that she did not apply to the Department of Architecture at city hall expecting to be Gaudí. But this was wrong.

"You keep that in mind, missy," Sak-hee said, shoving the envelope into his pocket. "Gaudí only built those fancy cathedrals because the city council let him."

He brayed with laughter. He-jin faltered. She thought of the four years she spent studying to land here. She forced herself to laugh along.

He-jin threw her bag onto her bed and struggled to get her shoes off. The door swung shut behind her. Goshiwon doors rarely opened outward, which was against building regulation. But that was what sold rooms. Goshiwon residents scrimped and saved, only buying what was necessary. Privacy was not one of those things. Both kitchens and bathrooms were communal. The room, however—

that was yours and yours only. Naturally they wanted doors that opened inward, a way to slip into the room without revealing to the world how you lived.

It wasn't just the doors; Hanmaeum violated a host of other building regulations. He-jin found something funny about it, at the fact that a Department of Architecture employee lived in a building that wasn't up to code.

He-jin's room was in the corner of the hallway, the goshiwon equivalent of a penthouse. The extra 40,000 won per month meant that she got a window, a tiny 40 cm by 30 cm pane of glass. The only view it provided, however, was that of a concrete wall. There was a time when He-jin could look out the window and see trees. Over the years, a thicket of half-built buildings and foundations had sprouted up around He-jin's goshiwon, surrounding it.

Regardless, a window meant ventilation. During monsoon season, He-jin left the window open to listen to the rain until the frame would swell with moisture, forcing her to rattle it with all her strength to unstick it.

She looked around her home, all 4.5 square meters of it. A corner was occupied by a stack of textbooks that she never bothered to get rid of. Another several feet were taken up by the bed, which was little more than a folding mattress. All of it was packed under the desk to make room when she wasn't sleeping. He-jin thought about texting Jin-ee to ask whether she was still up but decided against it. She was probably studying.

She lay down on her bed instead and looked up. She could see the scribbles and etchings left behind by previous tenants.

Third time is the charm, one of them read.

Wasn't for me, read the one below.

The one in the left corner read, *So-hee and Jun-hyuk forever,* accompanied by a heart. Right below, *What kind of a restudy has the time to date?*

He-jin ran her fingers over one of the scribbles, carved into the plywood with a knife. *4 years 2 months and 11 days.*

He-jin woke up feeling well-rested. She even luxuriated in that feeling for a while before she realized what that meant.

"Shit."

She reached for her glasses and phone, which read 8:34 a.m.

"Shit," she said again, bolting up to get dressed, "Shit, shit, shit."

It was fifteen past nine when she got to the city hall. Thankfully, Sak-hee was out of the office. She hurried to her cubicle and sat on her chair, breathing out a sigh of relief. Her phone buzzed and she looked down. Two texts from Jin-ee.

You weren't there at the study cafe today.

And then: *Lunch at the usual spot?*

The rest of the morning was a blur of paperwork. He-jin organized all the documents into different piles, pushed one of them in the corner with a noise of derision, and began working. She signed off on the clearing of several illegal plywood houses, and then examined a renovation proposal.

But eventually she could put it off no longer. With a sigh, she began rifling through the pile of construction proposals, sorting them into three neat piles.

1. Harmless, well-meaning projects that dotted the i's and crossed their t's.

2. Projects not up to code.

3. Projects not up to code (but were backed by big companies).

The third pile went directly to Sak-hee. *Protocol*, he called it, using his favorite word.

She stared at the pile. What would happen if she rejected everything in pile three? How would Sak-hee react if she took a hammer to it all, all those polite coffee sessions and hefty envelopes?

A light tap on her shoulder jolted her out of her daydream.

"What, still working?" one of the senior assistants asked. "Let's break for lunch. Sak-hee is buying."

"What is it?" she asked, already knowing the answer.

"Galbitang."

"Sorry," He-jin answered. She narrowly avoided making a face. "I'm a little behind here. I'll be okay. I had a big breakfast anyway."

He shrugged and left to eat lunch at Sak-hee's favorite restaurant. It was the third time that week.

"Galbitang in this weather," He-jin said to herself. Her scalp itched with perspiration at the thought of the boiling soup. She craned her neck to make sure her colleagues were gone, then hurriedly gathered her things and left for lunch.

She was half a block away from the restaurant when she realized her mistake: She had forgotten to change out of her work clothes. He-jin thumbed her civil servant ID card. Her grainy photograph smiled back at her, but it seemed forced to her now. She unclipped the ID from the lanyard and shoved it to the bottom of her handbag. There was nothing to be done about her work blazer. She'd just have to hope Jin-ee wouldn't ask questions.

Gyeoul-bada was a seafood restaurant near her goshiwon. Sheets of paper taped to the windows advertised various menus. Fish roe stone pot soup for 8,000 won. Spicy braised pollack for 45,000 won. The rest of the menu was hidden behind a series of large fish tanks, each taller than the one behind it. There were no lids. The water filled the tallest tank and overflowed into the shorter ones in front of it, all of it ending up as a puddle on the concrete floor. There was no drain either. The puddle was simply allowed to grow. The air around the restaurant was heavy with the smell of brine. A languid hose refilled water into the brackish tanks. The total effect was something between the Hanging Gardens of Babylon and a beached whale carcass.

A large sea bass swam toward He-jin, its tattered fins dragging its heavy body along. It had that expression that all fish wore, jutting gray angles and vacant eyes, wide with eternal surprise—as if it could not believe the fact that it was a fish.

He-jin pressed the door button and waited for the automated glass pane to open. The thing slid open halfway, slowed down, and stuck fast halfway through. She gingerly slipped inside.

"He-jin," Jin-ee said loudly, "over here!"

The restaurant was practically empty. There was no need to shout; Jin-ee did so anyway. A middle-aged man emerged from the kitchen, stared at He-jin with large, baleful eyes, then turned to walk back in.

"I already ordered," Jin-ee told He-jin. "I got you the eel rolls. I know you don't like the raw stuff."

He-jin found herself strangely touched at this slight gesture of consideration. Jin-ee was correct; she had wanted eel rolls. No one in the Department of Architecture knew what He-jin enjoyed, much less ordered it for her.

The food arrived before long. Jin-ee ate with one eye to her printed list of test questions. He-jin quietly picked at her food. She wanted to say something, anything—but nothing came to mind. Conversation with Jin-ee, something that had once been so easy, eluded her.

"Hey, how many different types of structural failures are there?" Jin-ee asked.

"Five," He-jin mechanically answered.

Jin-ee put her chopsticks down, focusing on her stack of notes. Her brows furrowed. After a while, she made a noise of exasperation.

"I give up," she said. "There's corrosion, defective materials, structure not being designed correctly, and manufacturing errors, but I can't recall the last one."

"I think the last one is unexpected problems. Like human error," He-jin said.

"Damn it. That's what it was," Jin-ee said. "I do not know how you failed the last civil service exam. You actually know this stuff."

He-jin laughed guiltily and shifted in her seat. He-jin hadn't failed. It was the entire reason why she could now work at city hall. Jin-ee didn't know. The clatter of their chopsticks quietly echoed in the empty restaurant. After a while, He-jin finally thought of something to say.

"Jin-ee," she asked. "Why do you want to do this? Be a civil servant?"

"It's a stable, respected job." Jin-ee answered without looking up from her notes. "Duh."

"No, I mean, beyond that," He-jin said. "Why architecture? I mean, who cares about zoning permits and building codes?"

"Well, why do you want to do it?" she asked back, her eyes still fixed onto the stack of papers.

There was a time when He-jin had an answer. Now, however, all she could do was sit and stare at the top of Jin-ee's head.

"Never mind," He-jin eventually said.

Jin-ee looked up, concern in her face. "Do you feel like you're burning out?"

"No," He-jin said, shaking her head. "Forget it. It was a dumb question."

"Seriously, you can tell me."

"Jin-ee, I'm not burning out."

"Okay. Because we can't quit now. I'm sure we'll make the cut next year. I'm sure of it. And then—"

And then what? He-jin wanted to ask. What if there was no *and then?* What if *and then* just ended up being a cubicle where you didn't belong, and everything you had done amounted to organizing proposals so your boss could tell which ones would lead to under-the-table deals? What if you had done all of this for backroom gossip and bad instant coffee and kidney stones from too much overtime?

He-jin tried to dip a roll in soy sauce and ended up drowning it. She ate it anyway, the salt parching her mouth.

He-jin sat alone at a bar and watched people slowly trickle in. Two days ago, the list of people who passed the first round of the civil service exams were announced. He-jin did not bother looking at the acceptance list; it wasn't the one that Jin-ee was studying for.

She wasn't here to drink; it was mostly to people-watch. Bars were always packed after test results came out. Those who made the cut celebrated. Those that failed still showed up, hoping to distract themselves with the drinking.

They're here to celebrate, He-jin thought, looking at the ragtag group of men who just entered the bar, asking for something with bubbles.

That one isn't, she thought, staring at the young man cradling his drink.

She was, in fact, so absorbed in her guessing that she did not notice the bartender approaching to refill her water.

"So, which one are you?" the bartender asked. "Celebrating or moping?"

"Aren't you taking a risk by asking that?" she answered, smiling.

"Well, you're smiling, so clearly you passed," he said. "My risk panned out."

"Sorry to disappoint, but I'm still studying for next year," He-jin lied, then regretted it.

Why had she done that? It wasn't like with Jin-ee. There had been no reason to lie.

"That's fine," the bartender answered. "I used to be a restudy too."

"Really?"

He-jin scrutinized the man with newfound interest. But he did not seem any different. He was slightly older than He-jin, dressed in a pair of worn slacks and a button-up.

"Stuck it out for three years before I eventually caved," he said. "My dad wasn't too happy about it, but I'm okay with how it all turned out."

"Are you?" she asked, then clarified. "Sorry if that sounded shitty. I was genuinely asking."

"No, it's fine," he said. He leaned back against the bar to watch the crowd, then shrugged. "I mean, it's a living, no?"

"It is," she said, then repeated herself, worried that she did not sound convinced of what he said. "It is a living."

The man appraised her for a bit.

"It's funny how similar the reactions are sometimes," he said. "Whether you make the cut or not."

"What do you mean?" He-jin asked.

"I've seen everything from crying to chucking their textbooks out the window," he laughed. "The funny thing is that it could be either-or. I can't tell if they got in or not."

He-jin laughed.

"That's true," she said. "Once, a girl two doors down from me took all of her notes and burned them in a bonfire. I was so sure that she had gotten in. A week later, she was writing up all those notes again."

They both laughed. He poured her a drink.

"On the house," he said, then added, "Well, there's actually a surefire way of knowing.

"If you make the cut, you leave the goshiwon. You get the hell out."

He-jin felt a stab of guilt. The bartender wasn't wrong. Goshiwons were, by design, a stopgap solution. Everything from the lack of deposits to the furniture: temporary. At the end, you left, for one reason or another.

"Sometimes I'd think that they became ghosts," he said. "The way they'd just up and vanished."

It was the other way around, He-jin thought. The people in the goshiwons were the ghosts. It was a pale half life, waiting for the acceptance notifications so that you could start your life in earnest. She had gotten out. Made the cut. All she had to do was enjoy her win; wasn't this supposed to be the easy part?

Her phone was dead by the time she stumbled out of the bar, but she could tell that it was late. The city was still in full swing. Karaokes and flashing neon lights blurred against gray concrete. Taxi drivers squatted on the curbside and swapped stories and cigarettes, waiting for the drunks to start filing out.

A man in a flimsy suit loudly accosted He-jin and she stiffened, her hand gripping her keys. She had heard somewhere that keys could be used as a makeshift self-defense weapon.

"Hey, where are you going?" he asked. "It's Friday. Come inside and have a drink."

He-jin squinted at the bar he was pointing at. A garish LED sign read: *Geumnam Best Host Bar.*

Relief flooded her. It was just a waiter for a host bar. Many such places dotted the area, bars that straddled the thin line between legitimate establishment and illegal sex work. He continued to speak, rattling off the words at a breakneck pace.

"I promise you won't regret it," he said. "Live a little! It's fifty thousand won for a table, another fifty to seat someone cute next to you. We've got some real lookers. Every bottle after the first is ten percent off. We've got it all, you name it. Chivas Regal, Ballantine's, Royal Salute, Johnnie Walker. We've got Johnnie Walker Black, Double Black, Green, Blue, you name it, we got it."

The man's bow tie was lopsided. It bounced precariously on the crumpled collar every time he emphasized a word. He-jin wanted to reach out and grab it, although she did not know if she wanted to fix it or strangle him with it.

"No," she said, slurring her words. "No, thank you. I've got to go home."

She waved down a cab, leaving the disappointed man behind. He called out after her, but it was unintelligible.

"Hanmaeum goshiwon," she said. The nightlife blurred behind her as she rested her head against the cool glass of the window.

They did not live in the same goshiwon, although He-jin had seen Jin-ee around the libraries and study cafés. But it was at Gyeoulbada that they first spoke.

She had been eating lunch alone. When she saw the woman get up from her corner and walk toward her, she groaned internally. She liked this restaurant because people from the goshiwon could rarely afford seafood.

Not that I can, she thought and considered her lunch, which was the cheapest thing off the menu.

"Hey, He-jin, right?"

"Yes," she answered. "How do you know my name?"

Jin-ee wordlessly gestured at the textbook next to He-jin's bowl. *Advanced Architecture & Design*, the title read. Next to it was He-jin's name, written in Sharpie.

"You want to go study together after this?" Jin-ee asked. When He-jin vacillated, she added, "I'm studying for the same thing."

He-jin searched the other woman's face for any hint of competitiveness but found none.

"Come on," Jin-ee said, smiling. "Let's study together. No hard feelings if you get in and I don't. I promise."

When He-jin awoke, she was still in the taxi. An old-fashioned song was playing on the radio, a pop number from the seventies. She looked out the window and realized with shock that they were on the wrong side of town. In fact, it was a different municipality entirely. She stared at the driver's reflection with naked terror. Where was he taking her?

"Hey," she said. "Where is this?"

"Miss?"

"Where the fuck are we going?"

"Huh?" The driver squinted back at her as if she'd asked a trick question. "Hanwoori goshiwon."

"Han*maeum*." He-jin replied, her panic ebbing into irritation.

"It's Hanmaeum goshiwon."

He-jin accepted the driver's apology with a vague nod and looked out the window again.

Municipality H was not a nice neighborhood. Most of the homes were built on the large mountain that dominated the area. They were old, beaten-down houses with corrugated tin roofs and PVC piping, most built immediately after the country was liberated. They called them moon towns, although no one really knew exactly why. Some said it was because the houses were close to the moon. Others said it was because the inhabitants went looking for work in the early hours of dawn while the moon still clung to the sky.

The man drove quickly, perhaps because he felt bad. The cheap plywood houses grew more and more scarce. He-jin looked behind her, staring at the mountain that rose into the night sky like some lumbering beast. She imagined wading into it, clambering past the chicken wire fence and disappearing into its belly. Beyond the jurisdiction of any goshiwon, municipalities, or city hall departments.

"Do you ever get homesick?" He-jin asked abruptly. "For places you've never been to?"

"What?"

"You spend years trying to open one door, convinced that what's on the other side is what you love—need, even. But when you open it at last, you just find more doors. Now, I see places and people that I've never known—and I think that I'd be able to love them," she said. "At least love better than what I know now."

The car's clock read 5:07 a.m. He-jin craned her neck. She wanted to see the sun rise beyond the large mountain. She wanted to see something beautiful and impossibly large, something she had once associated with architecture.

But it did not rise, long after the mountain dwindled into a lump of darkness.

The next day was more overtime. By the time He-jin made it back to the goshiwon, Soo was nowhere to be seen.

Small mercies, she thought. She was in no mood for his brand of nosiness tonight.

The first thing she noticed was the smell of smoke. She began to cough. Then she noticed the light. One of the rooms was open; the sallow light flooded the hallway. When she walked further, she saw a figure standing outside the open door. It was Soo.

"Fuck," he said, over and over again. "Oh fuck, fuck, fuck, fuck. Oh fuck."

He glimpsed He-jin and called out to her, desperately waving his hands. "Hey," he shouted. "Hey, over here!"

He-jin eyed him warily. "What is it?"

"Please," he said. Something about the *please*—a word she could not imagine coming from the man's mouth—made her reconsider. "It's 4B."

It took a moment before she realized that Soo was referring to a resident by their room number. Peering around Soo, she saw a man lying on the floor, the room hazy with smoke.

"I heard him screaming on the phone with his parents this morning, and then I saw him coming back with all these coal briquettes." Soo stood over the man and babbled. "And when I knocked, he didn't answer, so I used the master key, and he was like this and I didn't know what to do."

"Did you call the EMS?"

"Yes but they said wait and—"

"Well, call them again," she shouted. "And apply first aid or something."

"Is that what you do?" Soo wailed. "Is he dead?"

He-jin pushed past him, snapping over her shoulder. "Just get out—just call the hospital."

He-jin crouched over the prone man, 4B, and began clumsily pressing at his chest. The man's eyes flickered, perhaps jolted by the pain of He-jin pressing down on his ribs. He-jin's pulse thundered in her ears. Everything seemed far away, unreal. She blew air into his lungs. The man's breath reeked of soju. He-jin began reciting architectural information to distract herself from gagging.

What were the five reasons for a structural failure? She could not remember. Why did things have to collapse? The man made some sort of gurgling noise, and she had to look away. She did not know his name; only the number of the room—4B. Guilt roiled within her, followed swiftly by anger. It was unfair. Why did she have to feel guilty about not knowing the man's name? It was customary for those at goshiwons to not interact. They were strangers at best, competition at worst.

"Don't do that," 4B croaked. He-jin flinched with surprise. There was no pain or anger in the man's voice; he almost sounded exasperated. He-jin hesitated, then resumed pumping his chest.

"Ow," he said weakly. "Stop that."

"I'm just trying to help."

"Don't, please, it hurts," he said.

"Don't talk," she said. "EMS will be here soon."

That seemed to get his attention. He attempted to get up, but only managed to weakly flail.

"No," he said, and for the first time, genuine panic entered his voice. "Don't do that."

He-jin just kept pumping his chest, even though the man was awake. It helped distract her.

"Eight years," he said. "I've been here eight years. Eight years to be a civil servant and I got nowhere."

"I'm just trying to help," she said again. "Just trying to help."

She did not know what else to say.

"What's that?" the man suddenly said and pointed. "That."

He-jin looked down and saw her city hall ID card, still in its plastic sleeve and hanging from her neck on a cord. Her mouth felt very dry.

"It's nothing," she said, but the man raised his body and gripped the ID with surprising strength, pulling her down to his level. He first stared dully at the grainy photograph of her smiling face, and then at her.

Huh, was all that came out of his lips.

"Look," she said. "I just—"

"Why are you here?" he asked.

She thought about running out the goshiwon. Still, her hand mechanically pressed away at his chest. She felt like something terrible would happen if she stopped. Except that was wrong—something terrible had already happened; as a matter of fact, it was happening right now.

"Why are you doing here?" the man asked. "Get out. Get the fuck out of here."

"Look," she said. "I just—I felt like I belonged here. Or I wanted to belong."

The man made a sound, but He-jin could not tell if it was a fit of cough or laughter.

"You know," he gasped, "I really really really didn't want this. I just didn't know another way to leave this place."

The man weakly stood up again. He-jin saw the fury in his eyes and thought for a moment he would strike her. But he spit on her instead, the saliva landing on her collar and trailing down.

"You don't belong here," he shouted. "We don't fucking want you."

Before she could respond, the EMS workers arrived and lifted him onto a gurney. He began to convulse and heave, but she could tell that this was how he wept.

The sashimi boat arrived. Delicate slivers of flesh, plated atop a bed of white radish. The servers pointed to each one and named them: tuna, rockfish, flounder, mackerel, and amberjack.

It was the monthly hoesik, and everyone in the department gathered at a nearby izakaya to eat dinner and drink themselves blind. It wasn't the sort of occasion that you backed out of, not without hurting your chances of promotion.

He-jin's head was swimming with alcohol. She eyed the raw fish, arranged to resemble petals. Deboned and sculpted. A flower made out of open wounds. There were many things that she did not like about sashimi, but more than anything, it was how it looked.

Flesh shouldn't come in straight lines, she thought.

For the fourth time, Sak-hee raised his glass in a toast. Everyone reluctantly followed suit. He-jin clinked her glass with her neighbor, her eyes fixed on her supervisor. The stain she had pointed out earlier in the week was still there. She raised the glass to her lips. This time, however, when she smelled the soju, all she could think of was the previous night. The man in 4B and his stinking breath. He-jin queasily put the glass back down and excused herself from the table.

Outside the izakaya, the night was cool. The heat had finally relinquished its hold over Municipality K. He-jin took shuddering gulps of air, the nausea alleviating a little. From her pocket, her phone buzzed.

hey, didn't see you at the library today either. hope your studying is going okay.

Without thinking, she dialed the number.

"Hello?" Jin-ee asked. "He-jin?"

He-jin froze.

"Hello?" Jin-ee asked again.

"Hey," He-jin said in a rush. "Hey, sorry if I distracted you from your studying. Honestly, I'm not even sure why I'm calling."

"He-jin, is everything okay?"

"Yeah!" He-jin said, feigning a chipper voice. "I'm just, I just had a bit too much to drink, I guess."

Jin-ee's silence radiated from the phone, expectant, and kind. Finally, unable to bear it, He-jin said the only thing that came to her mind.

"Have you—have thought more about it? Why you're doing all this?" He-jin pressed forward without waiting for a reply.

"I mean, forget about your parents. Forget job stability. Fuck all that. Why do you like architecture?"

There was another silence, this time pensive.

"I guess I want to look at a building and think *I helped in creating that*, you know?" Jin-ee said at last. "To be responsible for something lasting and beautiful."

"They'd never let you," He-jin said, her voice too quiet to carry over the sound of the traffic.

"Sorry?" Jin-ee said but He-jin had already hung up the phone.

Back in the restaurant, the hoesik was in full swing. One of the assistants was singing, using a spoon as a makeshift microphone. Disgust roiled within He-jin, although she could not tell whether it was aimed at herself, the people in her department, or all those pale, listless faces at the goshiwon.

"He-jin!" said Paeng, the senior assistant. His face was flush with alcohol. "Where have you been!"

"Where is Sak-hee," she said, ignoring his words. "Where the hell is Sak-hee."

And then came that old question: Is everything okay?

"No," she said, and the pleasure she felt on being able to finally say it verged on manic. "Nothing is okay. Nothing will ever be okay. *Where the fuck is Sak-hee.*"

"He's over there," Paeng stammered. "He's taking a call."

He-jin stormed in the direction Paeng pointed. She imagined all the things she would say, what she would unleash on Sak-hee.

She found him near the bathroom, his back to her. She grabbed him and roughly wheeled him around. But when their eyes met, she faltered, distracted by the sheer panic in his face.

Not. Now, he mouthed at her, then turned back to the phone call. He cradled the phone with both hands, as if it was a delicate and lethal device that could kill him at any minute.

"I'm so so sorry sir," he said. "No, no, no, please continue."

He laughed, the sound high and ingratiating. No different than the laugh she had squeezed out in front of Sak-hee the first time they met.

He incessantly nodded his head the entire time. He-jin noticed his bald spot bob, but the urge to hit it did not follow. She stared at the man and tried to see what she always saw in him. The source of her misery and dissatisfaction, the reason why her work felt meaningless. The only thing in front of her was frumpy middle management, walking on the same eggshells on which she walked.

Her anger drained from her; nothing took its place.

She walked and walked. Someone in a side alley leaned against the wall and vomited with a ferocity. *Come here for a minute,* he said, and she scampered away. Later, two teenagers shiftily eyed an unattended motorcycle. A woman ran out of a bar with a man hot on her heels. *C'mon baby don't be like that,* he said. *Fuck you,* the woman screamed. A couple collided with another man and the three immediately began to shout, *watch where you're going* overlapping with *who the hell do you think you are.* More men in cheap suits luring tired white-collar workers with the promise of whiskey. *The best girls in town,* a man said. *Not very likely,* answered a tired-looking man but walked in anyway. A fistfight between two drunks. People peering outside the gray buildings to watch, their pale faces pouring out of the concrete wall like blind grubs. He-jin looked up, but she could not see the sky, blotted out by empty, grasping fingers of concrete, rebar, and fiberglass.

"We're closing in an hour," the man at Gyeoul-bada told He-jin.

"That's fine," she said, sinking into the wooden chair. Her feet burned with exertion. "I just need to catch my breath."

"You still have to order something."

"Okay," she said. "Whatever is fine."

"The knifejaw sashimi is good."

He-jin was about to tell the man that she did not eat raw fish before she changed her mind. Why not? What did it matter now?

"That sounds fine," she said. "And a glass of water please."

The alcohol was wearing off and exhaustion was setting in. From the kitchen, she could hear the man preparing the fish. There was a repeated and awful crunch, what she assumed was knife severing spine. She blearily leaned back on the chair and waited for what seemed like an eternity, but neither fish nor water arrived.

"Hello?" she asked. Her voice echoed in the empty restaurant. The sound of bones snapping continued. She looked toward the kitchen and saw a puddle of brackish water growing larger by the minute.

"Hello?" she asked again. But the only answer she received was that sound, growing louder and louder until it became a hammer beating a tattoo inside her skull. She clenched her eyes shut and pressed her hands into her ears, but the sound seemed to be coming from within her, radiating outward.

When she opened her eyes, she was on the cutting board. A gargantuan hand reached for her, grabbing her face. The fingers reeked of equal parts brine and cheap dish soap. He-jin dry heaved.

The five reasons for a structural failure are, boomed a voice from somewhere above her head.

Human error, human error, human error, human error, and human error.

With each repetition, the voice warped and bucked like water-logged timber.

First it was Soo's voice, then Jin-ee's, which became Senior Assistant Paeng's which in turn became Sak-hee's. And then it was 4B.

He-jin screamed and thrashed, but the hand firmly held her in place. The other hand lowered another fish next to her, one as large as she was. The fish opened its mouth and gurgled at her.

"You know," it sloshed, "you aren't what I expected. What fish tank did you graduate from?"

The knife swung, severing the fish's head. Warm, briny flecks of blood hit her cheeks. He-jin screamed again but the sound was drowned out by the thud of the knife.

Still, the severed head continued to speak.

"You keep that in mind, missy," it said. "Gaudí only built those fancy cathedrals because the city council let him." The head began to laugh and laugh. "And there's no way we'll let you do that! Not now, not ever!"

The knife sang downward—this time directly aimed at He-jin's neck.

He-jin awoke to something wet streaming down her face. Her phone was ringing. It was Paeng.

"Ms. Jeong," he said. "*Where* are you. It's nearly noon. It's a shitshow here. Sak-hee is furious."

He-jin jumped up. Her head throbbed.

"I'll—I'll be there in thirty minutes," she said. "I'm so sorry."

When He-jin arrived, however, Sak-hee did not have much to say aside from a terse reprimand. His frustration, it seemed, stemmed from elsewhere. Once back in her cubicle, she conspiratorially leaned over and asked another worker what was going on.

"It was all over the news. Apparently, a building burned down."

"What?"

"Yeah, some goshiwon. At least ten dead."

He-jin's pulse thundered in her ears. Her colleague's voice sounded fuzzy, as if it was coming from a great distance, or through a body of water.

"It's a clusterfuck," he said. "The building had a dozen fire code violations, but someone from this office rubberstamped it."

"What goshiwon," she said.

"Huh?"

"Which goshiwon collapsed?"

"I don't know—why does that matter?"

He-jin fished out her phone, her heart thundering.

Please no, she thought as she dialed Jin-ee. *Please, please, please, please no.*

There was no answer. He-jin began to run, already calling again.

"Where are you going?" he called after her.

It was easy to find the remains of the building. The parents of the dead students had formed a crowd around the block. Someone had framed the faces of the dead and placed them outside the ruin in a neat row. She scanned their dead faces, smiling and vacant, but Jin-ee's was not there.

"Excuse me," she said to an officer who stood nearby. "Is this everyone? Everyone who died, I mean."

"We don't know," he said. "The rubble is still unstable and we're having trouble getting inside." He gestured to the remains of the building. "Are you family?"

"No, I'm—"

What was she?

She realized she didn't know where Jin-ee lived. She looked again at the photographs of the dead. What was she to these people? To Jin-ee? The voice of 4B echoed in her ears. *Get the fuck out. You don't belong here. We don't want you.*

In the end, He-jin walked away alone to the only place she could think of. And when Gyeoul-bada's automated doors did not slide, she gripped them with her hands and shoved them open. She walked in, prepared to wave away the menu. Impossibly, she hoped that she would see Jin-ee there, sitting at her usual spot.

But she was not there. Nothing was there. The restaurant was gutted, the tables gone, a few chairs upturned in the corner. She walked outside. The tanks, too, were empty. He-jin noticed a piece of paper taped to the door she'd missed in her hurry to get inside.

Closed indefinitely.

He-jin walked back into the restaurant and sat on one of the chairs, the same one she sat on last night. Or had that been a dream?

Without the furniture or lights, the restaurant felt hollow, the small space cavernous. He-jin sat there for a while, until she noticed a humming from the kitchen. When she looked through the porthole window of the kitchen doors, she saw another fish tank. This one was still running. Fish filled it to the brim. They began to thrash around, as if they could sense that she was watching. More water spilled out of the tanks. Fin and flesh, shades of mud and ochre, churned and roiled. Tattered gills sucked in dirty water; their eyes remained fixed on He-jin. She backed away and tripped over an upturned chair.

She lay where she fell, quietly gasping. Still, she could hear the sound of the water, of bodies thudding against glass.

What would happen to the fish in the tanks, she wondered. All those blank, dead faces, suspended in the dark.

ACKNOWLEDGMENTS

Sincere thanks to the editors of *Barnstorm* for publishing the short story "Autophagy."

AN CHANG JOON was born in Seoul, Korea, but raised somewhere between Uzbekistan, Korea, and the eastern coast of the United States. His writing explores borders, not as a flat line, but as a liminal space of their own. His prose can be found in *Barnstorm* and *Blue Earth Review*, and he was the runner-up for the *Gulf Coast Review*'s 2022 and 2023 Fiction Contest. He is the Korean translator for Nellie Hermann's novel, *The Season of Migration*.

Sarabande Books is a nonprofit independent literary press headquartered in Louisville, Kentucky. Established in 1994 to champion poetry, fiction, and essay, we are committed to creating lasting editions that honor exceptional writing. With over two hundred titles in print, we have earned a dedicated readership and a national reputation as a publisher of diverse forms and innovative voices.